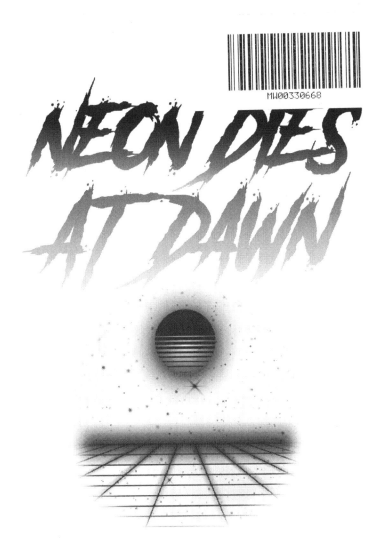

NEON DIES AT DAWN

ANDERSEN PRUNTY

GRINDHOUSE PRESS

To Carrie,

I know you're a bearded lady at heart. Grab your Speedo, we're grilling corn.

Also by Andersen Prunty

NEON DIES AT DAWN

THE THING LYING IN WAIT

The road is quiet. I hear the woman before I see her emerge from the shadows to continue wandering down the middle of the road. She looks young. Her clothes look like they were thrown on her in a hurry. She shuffles slowly, like she's woken from a night of being beaten or used roughly or maybe she's just out of her head on something. I'm not close enough to see her expression but I imagine it's blank and hollowed out. I've seen it on so many people before. It's almost standard issue around here. Whatever thing inside her that made her her is gone. I want to help because I have a gut feeling how this is going to turn out but I have to be careful because ... I have a gut feeling how this is going to turn out. I'm afraid. The kind of paralyzing dream-fear that makes it hard to move.

I need to get her off the road.

"Hey!" I yell.

She doesn't even turn. I may not have yelled that loud.

I've forgotten to turn on my porch light again.

I walk down the front porch steps, hoping she'll catch the movement, hoping the streetlights will illuminate me. A creepy older man in the middle of the night offers no solace for someone like her but she doesn't have to come to me. Could just as easily run in the opposite direction. The important thing is for her to get off the fucking road.

Closer now, I notice the collar around her neck, a chain trailing behind her, eaten by the darkness.

1

"Hey!" This time I yell louder. I'm sure of it.

My fear, my terror keeps me from going and grabbing her. This isn't paralysis. It's just common sense.

As if smelling that fear, the thing lying in wait roars to life.

The woman in the road responds to the growl of the black van's engine and she turns, the bright headlights blinding her, the van nailing her with a sickening impact. Her scalp arcs up into the glow of the streetlight and lands in the yard across the street. It barely makes a sound.

The van is already long gone, the face behind the wheel seared into my brain. I recognize that face.

The girl lies in a tangled mess on the sidewalk a few doors down.

My phone is already in my hand.

In the distance, the city is indifferent, its neon glow like some unblinking eye.

I should be shaken and traumatized but I'm not.

WORK

The sun sinks below one of the tallest buildings downtown. I'm on the back porch smoking a cigarette, avoiding the front yard. To cross into the front yard would bring last night back in all its screaming violence and that might unlock everything that came before that, and I don't have a therapist, but if I did I'm pretty sure they'd tell me those aren't good things to dwell on. Or they'd tell me I need to think about them more. That I need to purge them. Work through them. Work. My whole life has been work and just when I thought I was done with it, I'm not. If I'm going to do this, that's the only way I can really think of it. Going back to work. Doing a job.

I'm supposed to be retired.

The baby's cries come from the house.

I crush out my cigarette and go back inside.

There are a lot of things I didn't think I'd ever have to do again.

THE THINGS YOU LOVE

Kim Barrel will do just about anything for a thirty-pack of Hamm's beer.

"You got it?" she asks.

"It's in the refrigerator."

"I don't know why you can't just bring him to my place."

"He's more comfortable here."

The truth is that Kim's house is uninhabitable.

"You don't even got a fenced in yard so I can bring my dogs over. I gotta go back over and let em out."

"You live like five houses down."

"It's just a hassle, is all."

"You gotta do what you gotta do. Just don't be gone too long. I'll give you a key so you can lock up if you need to leave for a few."

Kim looks exasperated, says, "Why me?"

I try to give her a look as if to say does she really need to ask that question but like most people who live around here, myself included, she's not too bright, so I clarify.

"That Ken guy just showed up. I don't even think he bought that house. I think he just moved in. Danny's a convicted pedophile. Phil's on crack or something. Jerry and Kelly already have twelve kids and four grandkids living over there and I'm pretty sure half of them are feral. And you and I both know that Mary killed her husband. He didn't just 'fall down the stairs.' He was in a wheelchair. Since when do people in wheelchairs use the stairs? How did he even get upstairs to begin with? And I haven't seen Big John in six months."

Kim waves me away with a meaty arm and heads into the kitchen.

"Big Kim needs a beer," she says.

I go into Austin's room. He's sleeping in his crib. He's not going to be happy when he wakes up and I'm not there. I don't really have a choice. Technically, my sister has custody of him, but I take him most weekends. I could have told her I had plans this weekend but the less she knows, the better. I'm sure Kim's parenting skills are highly suspect, but she's managed to keep at least five dogs alive since I've known her, so there's that, at least. Maybe Austin will find her as amusing as I do. Maybe he'll come to a revelation I wish I'd come to at that age: Sometimes you just have to make do with what you get. Make the most of it. Because a kid like Austin? He's not getting much. Just like me, if he wants something, he's going to have to go after it and even then it's probably going to remain forever out of reach. Heaven forbid he manages to fill his life with people he loves. Because there's another lesson for him: The things you love will always leave you.

VICIOUS SLAUGHTERERS OF DESPERATE WOMEN

Full dark now and I barely know why I'm here. By car, it's only five minutes from my depressing neighborhood but it feels like a different world. I have a beard and a ponytail and dress the way I always have—t-shirt, jeans that fit, black boots—so I almost fit in except it feels like everyone in the Oregon District is thirty years younger than me.

I haven't drank since I was twenty-two and can't really say I've missed it. Quitting was a prerequisite for Ann to marry me. Looking back on it, I miss the naiveté I had then. This current version of myself says you don't ask someone to give up something they love and maybe I was too in love with drinking at the time. Or maybe Ann could see that if we went into our marriage as a three-some she'd probably be the bride I paid the least attention to. At least in the long run. Drinking doesn't make any demands. It would have been the quiet wife. The good listener. The one you told all your problems to. What neither one of us realized was that you always leave this world by yourself. Just like Ann was alone. Part of me was mad at her about that. I'd been at the hospital for two months, sitting by her bed even though she was on so much pain medication she was barely conscious, and she dies in the fifteen minutes I go down to the cafeteria to grab a sandwich.

Ann's gone but the beer's still here. It's everywhere.

And because this is Dayton, the bartender doesn't look at you like an alien when you order a Miller Lite.

I pay with cash and put the tip down. I don't want them to have a record of my name.

I take my beer to the smallest empty table I can find. Spend a few hours sitting at the bar and they'd remember my face, even though I'm a pretty forgettable guy.

I sit down and tune in to the conversation next to me, mainly because the woman has that kind of voice that cuts through everything. I try to not pay attention, but it's still there, hitting me in the sinus cavity and rolling around in my skull.

"He just drove by and I swear he said, 'I'm gonna fuck your dog!'"

A man sitting at the table says, "Why would someone say that?"

"I don't know!" the woman yells.

Another man at the table says, "I don't even know what that is. Is that, like, animal harassment?"

"Catcalling a dog?" the other man says.

"I'm gonna fuck your dog!" the drunkest woman at the table slurs.

And, like that, they've found their drinking mantra for the night. I'm able to mostly ignore their zigzagging conversation that seems centered around work, restaurants, and sports, but that phrase—I'm gonna fuck your dog!—cuts through the fog with laser precision and I make a note to ask Kim Barrel if anyone has ever said anything like that to her.

I sip my beer and look around the small bar. The patrons aren't really as young as I thought they were when I first came in. There are even a couple groups of guys around my age and I wonder if the fact that I'm alone will make me stand out more.

Every woman in the bar seems really appealing to me and I wonder if that's because I'm old and attracted to their youth or if it's because of the internet. Like everyone now has the tools to become the best versions of themselves. They don't have to figure anything out anymore. The answers are all right there. Here's what everybody else is doing and they're all talking about it all the time. Come and join us. You don't want to be alone, do you?

Or maybe it's just been so long since I've had sex that anyone looks good.

I look at a woman holding court with three men and she seems patently intimidating, all gleaming white teeth and glowing skin and bright eyes, and I wonder what I would possibly talk to someone like that about. Listening to me talk for more than two minutes would make her want to go home and shoot herself in the head.

Then I see what I came here for entering through a door at the end of the bar.

Kasey Rumble.

Young women really need to stay off the internet.

Especially when their dads are notorious drug dealers and probable pimps, vicious slaughterers of desperate women.

She affixes a black apron around her slender waist and I think, "A daughter for a daughter."

Someone shouts, "I'm gonna fuck your dog!"

REDUCED TO A THING

Kasey Rumble is twenty-five years old. Three years younger than my daughter, Ally, had been at the time of her death four months ago. Kasey lives in an apartment in the Belmont area of Dayton. Sometimes Kasey goes out to party when her shift at the bar ends, but usually she goes home. She's typically out of the bar by three. I know this because Facebook told me so. She likes to take pictures of herself in her car with the caption: "Exhausted." The reason she doesn't usually go out afterwards is because she's in a relationship with a woman who teaches for the Dayton Public Schools who's been busy readying herself for the coming school year, only a week away. I know the green Kia Soul in the parking lot is Kasey's because she took a photo of it when she bought it and didn't bother blurring out the license plate. I don't know this for sure, but I'm guessing she gets in said car, takes it up Fifth to Wayne then to Wilmington to her moderately depressing apartment complex. Even at this hour, there is nowhere along her route that could be considered remotely isolated. I need to get her alone. Somewhere without cameras. I feel like it would have been a lot easier to abduct someone twenty years ago.

Young women really need to stay off the internet but I'm glad they don't. At least in this case.

With a dad like Kasey's, you'd think she would be a little savvier, a little more guarded. But she's probably been sheltered from the bad stuff. It's never the heroin dealer's daughter who gets hooked and strung out on the stuff. Nope. It's the daughter of the guy who works for twenty-five years in a paper factory.

Tonight, Kasey is going to leave work early to meet a woman named Nila Townsend who lives on the outskirts of Gethsemane, a rural town about ten miles west of Dayton. Because Kasey is trying to keep this from her girlfriend, she isn't broadcasting it all over social media. In fact, she's doing her best to make it sound like she's going to be at work really late and she can do this because the only people who really pay attention to her various accounts are her and her girlfriend. And, of course, me.

Nila Townsend is a nearly thirty-year-old woman, a veterinarian with various social phobias. She looks a lot like my daughter. And Nila Townsend doesn't exist.

Having hours of heartfelt conversation with Kasey online makes me feel kind of bad about what I'm going to do. But all I have to think about is Ally lying in the morgue, blue and purple and red and ripped apart, and I don't feel so bad. Ally had been struck by a car. More specifically, a van, I know now. I didn't need to wait for the toxicology reports to come back to know she had also consumed a nearly lethal dose of heroin shortly before her death. There had also been sexual activity. The report wasn't specific about how many men were involved. She wasn't raped, not that I thought she was. It's impossible to say no when you're nodding off, I'm assuming.

So now it's around ten o'clock and Kasey is talking to a male bartender behind the counter. She looks miserable and keeps touching her forehead and I feel the first sliver of confidence. She's really going to do it. Of course she is. Why wouldn't she? Nila Townsend is attractive and successful and the way she has with words makes it sound like this could be the most passionate relationship Kasey could possibly find herself in. Not to mention the kinkiest. Kasey's essentially mooching off her girlfriend anyway, so what does it matter if she loses out on a few hours of tip money?

Raucous laughter next to me. A chorus of "I want to fuck your dog!" and I take another sip of my beer and leave it half-full on the table and go out to my car and wait because I know that right now Kasey is telling the other bartender that she is not feeling well, that she needs to leave, that she will work next Friday and Saturday if she has to.

A few minutes later, Kasey comes out the back door of the bar and she's nearly beaming when she steps into the balmy summer night and hurries to her car and starts it up and I follow her, knowing she isn't taking her familiar route home. She is getting on 35 and taking the Gettysburg Avenue exit and I'm following her and after she turns onto Route 4 I'm overtaking her and putting distance in between us because I don't know who lives at the address I gave her—I just picked out something remote and impressive, with a 'No Trespassing' chain strung across the end of the driveway—and I'm going to be there waiting for her.

The navigator is telling me everywhere to turn but I'm not really listening to her because I've traveled this route so many times I'm pretty sure I know it by heart and when I finally reach the place I pull my car about twenty feet past the gravel drive, as far off the road as I can, before killing the lights. I'm nervous but it can't really matter. This has to work or I'm going to be in serious trouble before my plan can even get started. So I don't even let myself think about the consequences.

I wait behind a big catalpa tree and part of me can't believe it when Kasey pulls to the end of the driveway and stops. When she actually gets out of the car to approach the chain Nila told her would be unlocked but probably isn't. I don't even wait for her to figure that out though. That would have been the biggest indicator that Nila Townsend might not be what she really seems. I hit her with the stun gun and quickly wrap her mouth with duct tape. Then I just keep wrapping—arms, legs, ankles—before that panic-induced adrenaline can take effect and make her much stronger than her petite frame would suggest.

Within thirty seconds I've reduced her to a thing. She's not a young woman named Kasey. She's just Rudy Rumble's daughter and now I have her and she's, like, just a really heavy suitcase that barely manages to fit in the trunk of my car. Before slamming the lid, I dig around in the pocket of her shorts until I find her phone. I put it in my pocket and close the trunk.

I put a pair of gloves on, grab a hammer and a bungee cord I found on the road a while back. I pound the hook from the cord deep into her tire and reverse out of the driveway and about fifty feet or so in the opposite direction of my car. I turn it off and get out, lock the doors, realize I left the hammer on the passenger seat, unlock the door to retrieve it, see lights coming from way down the road, break into a full sprint to get to my car and I don't know what I'm trying to do. Get out before the headlights get here, I guess, because if they belong to a cop then I'm fucked but the speed limit on these roads is 55 and I am not that athletic so I'm just getting into my car when the other car zips past and, holy fuck, it is a Gethsemane police cruiser but, to my amazed surprise, it roars past and I don't see brake lights but I am shaking with nerves, knowing he's going to turn around, it's just taking him a second to process that what he just passed is not a normal situation. I try not to panic. I take deep breaths while waiting for the taillights to disappear. Then I turn my car on, reverse into the driveway and go back the direction I came from. A few miles down the road, I throw Kasey's phone out the window.

Back home, I pull my car into the garage. Kim Barrel is passed out in a sea of Hamm's cans and the baby is crying. I pick him up and walk around, trying to rouse Kim with my foot.

Finally, she comes to and says she needs to get back to her dogs and I think about shouting "I'm gonna fuck your dog!" but manage to restrain myself.

When Austin finally stops crying, I put him down and go retrieve Kasey from the car. She tries to yell but I did a great job with the tape and her voice is muffled. She tries to squirm and wriggle but it doesn't do much good. The garage is connected to the house so it's easy enough to get her in and down to the basement and into the cage I've spent the last month constructing.

A CAGE IN THE BASEMENT

The cage is bolted to the floor and there are two sets of handcuffs clasped to the inside. Building the cage filled me with a great sense of purpose and forward momentum, like I needed something to occupy my time when not taking care of Austin, which was most of the time. Building the cage was my way of dealing with the rage I felt at the necessity of my *ever* having to take care of Austin. When Austin was there it wasn't because I was just occasionally babysitting. Ally was not coming to pick Austin up. Would never come to pick him up. So I went to work on the cage as if I could put bars around the sense of emptiness that gave me.

Now that the cage actually contains a human, I'm filled with a sense of terror and revulsion.

Kasey is balled up in a corner of the cage, fully awake, shaking. She's pissed herself. After noticing the puddle and the stain on her shorts, I can smell it, dank and acrid in my otherwise very clean basement.

I stare at her sweating in the bright fluorescent light and feel genuinely bad for her but I have to remind myself why she is here.

I move closer to the cage, letting the stink envelop me.

"Do you know why you're here?" I ask.

She doesn't struggle with the tape, doesn't make any sort of dramatic gesture at all. Maybe she's already resigned. She shakes her head.

"Do you have any idea who I am?"

She shakes her head again.

13

I'm trying to sound calm but I'm as nervous as she is, maybe almost as scared. I awoke that morning with the realization I'd committed a crime. I'd abducted a woman. The authorities would not respect my rationale for committing that crime. They would only look at the crime that had been perpetrated, the crime committed by me, not all the crimes that had led to this one.

"I'm not sure how I should deal with this," I say. "I want you to know I feel terrible for what I've done. I know you're going to need basic things. You're going to need cleaned and fed and watered. But part of me wants to let you lie in your own filth. Part of me wants to let you starve. Because I know what the end result is going to be. I wish it didn't have to be this way. I really do." It feels like I'm talking a lot. This is probably more than I've said to anyone in a really long time. I'm starting to relax a little. This girl can't hurt me. For the moment, I have all the power and I try to let myself fully embrace that fact. I move closer to where she's balled up. "Let me tell you what I'm planning to do and then I'll take off your tape and you can tell me if you have any better ideas. Sound good?"

She just stares at me like I'm a crazy person and I have to remind myself this is probably a lot for someone in her situation to process.

"Just nod your head for yes and shake it for no."

She shakes her head.

I haven't really planned on this.

"What . . . what are you saying no to?"

She tries talking against the tape.

I shake away the impending confusion from my head.

"You know what?" I say. "It doesn't really matter if it sounds good to you or not. Before I tell you what I'm planning, I want you to know I don't *want* to do it. It's just something that has to happen. You're probably going to think I'm a very sick person but I am not the one who set this chain of events into action. You're going to want to blame someone, naturally. So I want you to know you have your father to blame. He's the reason for everything that's going to happen to you. I had a daughter once, too. Her name was Ally. Since coming into contact with your father, she got strung out on heroin. I guess she'd been a little depressed after having the baby. I'm sure it didn't help that her mother died a couple years before that and her husband killed himself while she was pregnant. It was accidental, but he still willingly took the stuff that killed him. Some people would say 'accidental overdose' sounds better than 'suicide' but I think it sounds really clumsy, you know? Suicide sounds like a choice made by a decisive person. Either way, it's a tragic fucking story. I'm getting off track. We were talking about my daughter and her heroin problem. It got so bad she started selling herself to pay for her habit. I didn't even know she had a problem until I got the call to bail her out. I was very shocked to find she'd been booked on a prostitution charge. A little part of me died that day. I mean, I'd never seen myself as a stellar parent, but I'd also never really thought I'd failed completely. After that she just kind of . . . disappeared. I couldn't really go looking for her because I was here taking care of her son. Every day felt like three, you know? Every minute was excruciating. You know how it is when you're waiting. Like you're there standing at the door, ready to go, and you have to wait for someone to find their keys and their phone, put on their shoes. Feels like it takes forever, doesn't it? Waiting is painful. Especially when what you're waiting for is your daughter to come home or to get *the call*. The call is not going to be anything good. It's going to be to say she's either in jail again, in the hospital, or in the morgue. I got the latter, unfortunately. She'd been hit by a car. Actually, a van. You probably know which one I'm talking about. Nobody saw it, but I know exactly what happened. She couldn't pay her dealer anymore. She was probably too strung out to be able to work it off by selling her body or, fuck, I don't know, maybe some other girl got jealous and turned against her. Regardless, she stopped being a person. Not even a customer or an employee. A toy. That's what she became. Your dad was good to her, though. He shot her up one last time before he and his friends had another go at her. Then they dumped her out of his black van and told her to walk down the middle of the road. They put a shock collar on her and attached it to the front of the van with a chain. They gave her a head start and if she started to wander off the road they gave her a buzz. Then they drove the van into her and drove away. The shock collar ripped her head off. I try not to think about what went on in the van. Were they laughing? Having a great time? Did they have hard-ons? Was it the kind of thing where the sheer sadism of the act turned them on? I just don't know. I have a lot of questions and I'm not sure I want them answered because I'm afraid the answers would be too painful. But I can't just sit around and do nothing. So this is what I'm gonna do. I'm going to shoot you up with heroin. I haven't decided if I'm going to let random guys fuck you or not. Outsiders might interfere with my job. I can't drive over you myself. Wouldn't get the pleasure out of it your dad does. So I'm pretty sure I'm just going to get you wasted and let you out on a busy highway and just hope somebody does the job. I mean, that's my plan for now. There might be some, uh, logistical alterations. I'm not going to ask if any of this sounds good to you because I'm sure it doesn't. I just want to know if you have any better ideas."

I put my hand through the cage.

"Bring your head over here so I can take the tape off."

She sticks her face out to me and I rip the tape off her mouth.

She doesn't have any better ideas. Only screams.

MY SISTER LISA

Lisa's house is clean to the point of sterility. We're in the kitchen. Her two grown daughters are in the living room playing with Austin. Her ability to keep her own children alive is one of the reasons I opted to let her have custody of Austin. Also, if it had gone to court, she would have won anyway.

She takes a sip of her coffee and looks at me with the disappointment she seems to reserve only for her daughters and me.

"I told you. I have a girl locked in the basement and I just don't think he should be around it. I mean, a crime is being committed."

"You're so full of shit." She adjusts her ridiculous wig with a delicate push of her plump hand. "The only crime being committed, if I had to guess, is that you're trying to move some stupid girl in."

"It's nothing like that. I think I just need some time to think. I haven't really taken that."

"I think having Austin there is good for you. *Especially* if there's no one else."

"Good for *me*, sure. But how is it good for him? I mean, I can feed him and clean him all right. I talk to him all the time. But that's about all I know how to do. Ann pretty much handled Ally's upbringing. You know that. I just went to work and made some money."

"You're not thinking about killing yourself, are you?"

Now it's my turn to give her a look like "Seriously?"

She throws her hands up. "I have to ask! He lives here so, obviously, it's okay if you don't want to take him, but he is going to need you in his life."

"I know. I'm not disappearing. Just taking some time. That's all. *Really*. That's all."

"I understand." She takes another sip of her coffee. "It's so easy to meet people online these days."

I roll my eyes. "After Ann died, I became a self-avowed monk. No offense to your gender, but you're all fucking crazy. I want my remaining years to be easy."

"If you don't come by I *will* send Harold out to check on you."

Harold is Lisa's husband.

"Dear god," I say. "Then I will want to kill myself."

"Oh, shut up," she says playfully.

"And just where is old Harold?"

"I don't know. Probably out fishing. Puttering somewhere. You know that's all he does since he's retired. Putters around. We don't go anywhere. Don't *do* anything. Of course, now that we have Austin, it's kind of impossible anyway."

And she goes on to talk about how boring and mundane her life is and it reaffirms my decision. This is what Austin needs. He doesn't need to be around me in the midst of a sadism hangover. He doesn't need to be there if I get caught or if something happens to me on one of my reconnaissance missions. Lisa only mentions her bout with cancer six times.

On my way home I'm wired and jittery from way too much coffee and I stop by a store to get the cheapest digital camera I can find and am not looking forward to the prospect of having to research how to transfer this shit to a DVD. Technology has always bored the piss out of me. Then I wonder what the point of it is. If I should even bother to document the process or just let Rudy Rumble figure it out. Let him have some of the unanswered questions I have.

The rest of the way home, I think about the woman in my basement and then, of course, I think about Ally and about what happened to her and wonder how anyone can watch that happen to a person. How they can even enable that happening to a person and I think I'm doing the same thing but have to stop myself and think, "No, this is different. This is way different." And it is, although part of me has to ask if maybe it's even worse.

BALANCE

"Finally done screaming?" I ask.

Kasey once again has her knees pulled up to her chest. Her make-up is smeared. Her face is red and blotchy. She doesn't answer me.

"Anyone come to help?"

She looks at me like "Duh."

"You happen to notice the soundproofing?"

Her eyes begin darting around the basement. Everything except the floor is covered in the spongy panels. They were gray when I bought them but I spray painted them white because I didn't want the basement to be more depressing than it already was.

"You ready to talk? You have any better ideas?"

"Just let me go." Her voice is hoarse.

"I can't do that. Believe me. I wish it had never come to this."

"Please just let me go. I can get Daddy to pay you something."

Her saying this hits me weird and I kick the cage. She's terrified. She scoots back into the corner with all the piss.

"What did I say that gave you the idea I was doing this for money?"

"I'm sorry. I'm sorry. I don't know what you want."

"'Sorry.' I guess that would be a good start. An apology. I've already told you what I want. Only, like I said, it's not really what I want. It's just the only thing I can think of that feels right."

"It's not right," she says.

I want to kick the cage again but I'm afraid it might not stop there. I'm afraid I'll open the cage, grab the chain hanging beside it, go in, and start swinging. And then it would be over too quickly. She would not have suffered enough. Rudy Rumble would not have the misery of speculating about her. Of wondering what happened to her. What *might be* happening to her.

"I don't know how I can best explain this to you. There is a balance to the world. In order to maintain that balance, corrective measures have to be made. Because we, as the human race, have not figured out perfection. We cannot do the things it would take of us to maintain this harmonious balance. My daughter should have never died in the first place. But it happened. And so a correction will be made. And I'm doing it in the way that feels most right to me. And I am the only person who matters to me anymore. Our prison system sends murderers to the gas chamber. All that does is remove one person from society. How does that correct any sort of balance? They don't let the family of the murdered hunt the killer. They don't punish the warped system that produced the killer—the bad parents, the bad neighborhoods, the failing schools, the shitty doctors who prescribe the shitty drugs, the sadistic peers. All of that is able to continue as it was. Nothing will get fixed. Nothing will get righted. Just one extra person removed from a sick society. And this is what people have voted for. This is the simplest solution. It's a symbolic corrective measure that only means something to the people who care."

"Hurting me isn't going to bring your daughter back. I'm real sorry for what happened to her but I didn't have anything to do with it, mister. I didn't even know her."

I have to take a deep breath to steady my rage. I know what she says is true but I didn't want to have my conviction challenged. Plus, she's totally missing the point.

"Please just let me go. I won't tell anybody what you did. I promise."

"I'm going to need you to tell me where your father lives."

"I can do that."

"Really? You're not going to protect him?"

She spits out a humorless laugh. "Why would I? Did you think I don't know what a piece of shit he is?"

I don't really expect her to say this. I go about setting up the camera I got. Make sure the entirety of the cage fills the viewfinder.

I want all of it to be visible but I don't want it to be so panned out the viewer would lose a lot of detail. But it can never capture all the details. All the details I want Rudy Rumble to sense. For instance, he's not going to be able to see that Kasey is so afraid even her eyeballs are shaking. He isn't going to be able to smell the fear sweat gathered in her clothes or the urine pooled around her. He won't be able to hear the hungry gurgle coming from her stomach. Then again, I didn't get any of that stuff when Ally went through whatever she went through. Sometimes the gaps the imagination fills in are even worse then the real thing.

I decide to not even turn the camera on. If I do get caught, why would I want a document of my madness? Maybe I can use it to send Rudy Rumble proof I have his daughter but whatever his diseased brain tells him is happening to her would probably be a lot worse than what I could actually bring myself to do. Maybe I should just return it.

Still, what Kasey said has me thinking and I continue fiddling with the camera so I don't have to say anything. Maybe my brain makes a hazy revelation about how I can use it but then panic floods back through me. Realistically, something needs to happen relatively quickly. It's unlikely the police are going to come beating down the door of a nondescript middle-aged white man with absolutely no criminal record and that's just it: I'm not a criminal. I'm not even incredibly bright. It's entirely possible mistakes were made. A heavy feeling drops in my gut when I imagine a CSI team swabbing my pint glass at the bar for DNA. It's an absurd thought, I know, but what if they come breaking down my door without me putting this daughter through one shred of discomfort? What if Rudy Rumble finds out about it? I don't know how he would, but Dayton isn't a big place and it would be entirely possible for someone as well connected as him to connect the dots.

I glance through the viewfinder. It isn't recording but she doesn't have to know that.

"I'm going to take the tape off you now."

I open a toolbox sitting on a worktable and approach the cage. I dig the blade of a pair of scissors in between the tape and the flesh of her arm and snip. I start pulling but she doesn't move.

"You're going to need to stand up and kind of twirl around so I can do this."

But she's . . . I don't know what she's doing. Pouting?

Should I offer the promise of food? Some reward to get her to do what I want? I don't want this to become that type of situation. After all, she isn't my daughter.

"You're going to make it easy for me to do this or I'm going to come in there and kick the fucking shit out of you. I may or may not fuck you in the ass if I do that. I've been a widower for coming up on five years. I could fuck a piece of wood at this point."

Who needs food as a motivation when you have fear?

She stiffly stands and turns in circles as I pull the tape off.

I ball it up and stick it in a trash bag. I won't throw any of this stuff away until this is over. I know what they can do with DNA and fabric samples and once all that shit's out at the curb it's not my property anymore.

"Now I need you to take your clothes off."

Perhaps I've overestimated my ability to instill fear because she isn't doing what I ask.

"Mister . . . please. You don't want to do this."

"I know there were a few gray areas when I laid all of this out to you before but I think I gave you a very clear picture of what was going to happen to you. It was a pretty big thing for me to kidnap you. I've never even thought about doing something like that before. Once I did that I became . . . invested, I guess you could say. So now I'm in this and I'm not going to do it halfway. Unfortunately for you, you're in this too. I'm not going to ask you to like it but I don't want you to get the wrong idea. I don't want you to have any hope. I don't want you to think, for a second, that this isn't real. Now take off your fucking clothes."

And this woman who will always be a girl to me, she's good. I thought she would just strip off her clothes and toss them out of the cage but she doesn't. She looks at me and says, "Point taken. But you really don't want to do this. You're not my father. You'll feel bad. It's already hurting you inside. I can tell."

And then she makes an almost insolent expression and locks eyes with me as she slowly pulls up her shirt. There's a brief second where the t-shirt is in front of her eyes and when it's over her head, she catches my eyes lifting up from her body and she knows she has me and I feel defeated and humiliated and concentrate to lock eyes with her as she undoes her shorts and slips them down her legs, unclips her bra and pulls it down her arms, slides her underwear down. I'm thinking I can look later and know I shouldn't be thinking this. Or, I don't know, maybe I should. I'm doing a terrible thing. What's the point of trying to convince myself I'm not a terrible person?

She kicks the clothes out of the cage and I unspool the hose and spray her down. Spray the puddle of urine away, put her clothes in the washer, and get back upstairs as quickly as I possibly can.

HANDSTANDS

In person, Rudy Rumble doesn't look anything like I imagined he would. I'd managed to find a photo or two online—he is, after all, Dayton's Parking Lot King—but they were studio photos that were probably taken a decade prior. It was barely enough to corroborate that his was the face I'd seen behind the wheel of the van. This is a man who has a tremendous amount of luck and success, much of it having to do with things on the edgier side of life. So I guess I thought he would look edgier. I don't know what I was hoping for. At least a leather jacket or something, I guess.

He looks like a dad.

A typical clueless Ohio dad.

His hair is graying and curly and he wears it in a baby mullet that was probably the new thing in his freshman year of high school. He's wearing a striped polo shirt tucked into a pair of denim carpenter shorts. He's wearing white socks and bargain tennis shoes. Maybe this is his way of being unassuming.

We're both in Handstands, a sports bar in a strip mall in Washington Township, a fairly affluent suburb just south of Dayton.

I'm here because I want to watch him decline the way I have declined. I've kept mine hidden pretty well but that's really only because there's no one in my life to observe it. There's Lisa, sure, but she's primarily self-involved, with ancillary attention paid to Austin, her daughters, and Harold.

Kasey told me this was where her dad hangs out most nights. She told me that after I removed one of her teeth and asked if she wanted me to keep going. She's not withholding information to protect her father. She still thinks there's a chance I'm going to let her go.

Rudy Rumble seems boisterous and affable and I'm not sure he knows his daughter is missing yet. There's a Reds game on the TV behind the bar and he and his three friends divide their attention between that, their beers, and passing around their phones, which seems to elicit either laughter or tongue-clicking, glowing praise. I'm trying to observe them without being obvious. Anyway, he doesn't seem to have the *weight* about him I think he should have if he knows Kasey is missing.

When I get home, I'm going to mail the tooth to him.

On my way home, I buy a staple gun and another push broom.

THE CLOSEST LIVING THING

I sit on my back porch and drink coffee and smoke cigarette after cigarette. The porch at the front of the house, the one from which I saw the girl get hit by the van, is the more utilitarian of the two. It's really more like a stoop. It's where a person who actually likes talking to their neighbors would hang out. The porch I'm on now runs along the back of the house and overlooks the distant city. My father-in-law helped me build it when Ann and I bought the place around thirty years ago. We bought it because of this view. And it was the best we could afford. And we didn't know the area well enough. If Dayton were New York, it would be a million-dollar view. But Dayton isn't New York and if I tried to sell my house tomorrow, I probably wouldn't get much more than what I paid for it.

Ann and I would sit out here a couple nights a week, at least. She'd talk and I'd smoke and we'd both look at the twinkling lights of the city, the neon blooms of purple and pink and green, and wonder what went on there. Neither one of us was really a city person. Crowds made me nervous and traffic made Ann nervous and we never really had the money to spend on a nightlife anyway. Still, the city was always there, providing a distant pulse, an ever-changing rhythm, to a long marriage that saw more than its fair share of stagnation. Buildings went up and came down. Lights came on and went off. Sirens wailed. Bands played. Crowds of people shouted and cheered. Helicopters circled. The city's corona of luminescence slowly expanded. It was a strange, almost abstract bond but sometimes it felt like the observation of these things was our common thread. It was there before Ally came along. It was there when she moved out. I've always needed some sense of purpose. Without Ann, the view doesn't seem to mean as much.

Christ. I miss Ann and Ally.

I try not to think about the girl in the cage, the closest living thing to me right now.

WAITING

I sit on the bottom step of the basement stairs and watch Kasey. I haven't washed her soiled clothes yet, haven't given them back, so she's naked. She's lying on her side, in the fetal position, and I think she's probably hungry. I have food upstairs but I'm not going to cook for her. You cook for people you love and I do not love Kasey Rumble. Same as with her dirty clothes. I will wash them when I've dirtied enough clothes to fill the washer. Or maybe I won't. Maybe if I need the room I'll take her clothes out and put them in the bag with all the other damning evidence.

I've deleted Nila Townsend's account from Facebook. Tried to anyway. It isn't as easy as I thought it would be. Anyway, I make it a point to not read through the messages Nila and Kasey exchanged. Made it a point to block all that out before acquiring Kasey. I don't want her to be a person. She can't be. She's a pawn. A tool. A canvas to exorcise all those really bad feelings I've been having the past few months.

I approach the cage.

"Roll over," I say.

She rolls over and I feel like she's being really dramatic, acting weaker and more pathetic than she really is. Blood is crusted to her chin from where I extracted the tooth. I fire up the hose and blast her in the face until all the flakes of dried blood are gone and I can't tell if the lower half of her face is red from the blood or the blast of water.

"I'm going to get you some food."

I drop the nozzle of the hose into the sink and I'm pretty sure she's lapping up water from the floor.

I keep waiting for this to feel good.

GARBAGE LOAF

The store where I walk to buy my cigarettes doesn't have much in the way of real food. It's mostly just overpriced junk food. They have a deli refrigerator with a bunch of pre-made sandwiches and some sad fruit. Then I see a shrink-wrapped, football-sized package labeled 'Garbage Loaf.' Sounds perfect.

I take it to the counter.

A young, skinny guy with massive earlobes puts down his phone to ring me up. I'm pretty sure he has an asshole tattooed on his forehead.

He picks up the package and turns it over in his shaky hands, looking for a barcode.

"I don't think nobody's ever bought this before."

I'm not sure if I'm supposed to respond or not. I squint at the garbage loaf, thinking that will help. Ask him for two packs of cigarettes. He puts down the garbage loaf with great relief, as though he's been temporarily pardoned from something. He turns back around with the cigarettes and we're right back to the same dilemma. There's a weird expression on his face, almost like horror, as he looks at the garbage loaf.

"I just don't know, man. No one's ever—"

"I know," I say. "No one's ever bought it before."

"That's right," he says. "Maybe it's something the Monarch brought in."

I don't know what he's talking about and wonder if I should just punch him in the throat and take it. The situation is so obviously confusing to the guy there's no possible way he could explain it to the cops.

He's holding the garbage loaf again, testing its heft.

"I guess I could call my manager," he says, but I can tell he doesn't want to do this. That, right now, that's one of the most dreaded things in the world to him.

"Look, man, I'll give you two dollars for it."

"You can probably just . . . take it? I mean . . . there's no barcode. Maybe it's something they were just gonna throw out or maybe . . . The Monarch." He's talking too much and the words are getting jumbled in his head.

"Sounds great." I pluck the garbage loaf from his hands and tuck it under my arm so he can turn his attention back to the cigarettes.

Back home, I slice off two pieces of garbage loaf and take it down to Kasey.

THE WEIRD SHIT

Rudy Rumble is at Handstands again. I'm sure he's received the tooth. I'm sure he knows Kasey is missing. Still, there is not the weight about him I had hoped to see. Tonight he's drinking with an older man with bleached blond hair who wears a pink belly shirt to expose a colostomy bag and another man wearing all black in a slightly Western fashion. His tan skin, coal black hair, and mustache make me think of Burt Reynolds except this man seems a lot bigger and fatter. As usual, they watch the ballgame and pass their phones around and drink.

Around eleven they all leave the bar.

I follow them. They don't notice me.

I see it in the parking lot and know immediately where they're headed.

The black van.

The blond guy gets sick in the parking lot but laughs it off. He empties his colostomy bag on the pavement and then takes a picture of it, the flash illuminating the three of them standing around it like old ghouls.

I get in my car at the edge of the parking lot and wait for them to pile into the van and pull out. I follow them.

They drive maybe a mile down the road and into another strip mall parking lot and I'm pretty sure I know what their destination is. Bedazzled, the all-nude gentlemen's club.

I can't follow them inside.

It's not anything moralistic. It's just impossible to go unnoticed in a strip club. The second you enter you are a mark. If you spend money, the girls will not leave you alone. If you spend no money, they will ignore you. But in order to ignore you, they have to first know who you are.

The van pulls around back and I decide to wait in front until I notice a police car camped out there, lights off. Either a crooked cop or the city's attempt to stop prostitution. Maybe both.

I pull around back, on the outer perimeter of the parking lot, and kill my lights.

The trio gets out of the van and enters the club through the back.

Now I'm super bored and know from experience I don't like the way boredom feels. I don't like where my mind goes. It wants to think about everything all at once and everything I can think about makes me really anxious or really sad.

I turn the radio on, open up a music app on my phone and it's playing through the car's speakers. There's an explanation for this but I prefer to think of it as magic. If not, I'll waste countless hours of my time absorbing technical manuals and service terms and conditions and I have a lot more important things I need to do. As per usual, I have it on its most random setting, skipping forward until it comes to something just alien enough to keep my attention. I glance down at the album artwork and it's white and pastel purple and looks cheesy as fuck but maybe also ironic and I don't really care because I like the way the music makes me feel. That's all music really means to me. This makes me think of a green field some time in the summer, morning maybe, after the dew has burned off, and somewhere there's white linen flapping in the breeze. Dry and clean. It makes me almost sleepy. I click on the icon that means 'more like this' and hope for the best.

To my left, a white box truck pulls up to the loading dock of one of the other stores in the strip mall. The driver gets out of the truck and walks around to the back of it. The side of the truck says 'DEEP' and I want to see that as some kind of metaphor for something but it's probably just a product name. The driver opens the back of the truck. The back door to the store opens and a woman emerges. The two of them begin unloading the truck and arguing in a language I don't understand. I think the people are Indian, so maybe it's Hindi. That doesn't help a lot. Not that I really want to know what they're saying anyway.

The current song finally ends and it shifts to one that is darker in tone. There's the sound of rain and some synthesized instrument and something about the song strikes me as vaguely Asian. Or maybe I just think that because the band's name is Vaguely Asian and I'm once again stricken with the solipsistic thought that the world is just some reflection of my own subconscious, which makes it really pleasurable on some levels and really masochistic on others. The music is taking me to a rainy night in a city like Tokyo or something and the Indian couple's fighting has wound down. The man leans against the truck and smokes a cigarette while the woman scrolls through her phone, and as I watch them, it's hard to convince myself it isn't raining.

I look at my phone, think about calling Kim Barrel and telling her I want to fuck her dogs before hanging up. But I don't. I don't even have her phone number. Would be surprised if she has a phone at all. I imagine her calling some kind of hotline for dog owners where she can just sit and listen to them bark on an endless loop for however long she wants, scratching or quieting that psychotic itch buzzing through her ironed-out brain.

I light a cigarette, lose myself in the music, and keep my attention on the black van.

That's the same van that killed my daughter. I know it is. It's hard to not want to destroy it. To stay in my car and not slash the van's tires or shatter its windows.

I swallow down some bile and take another drag from my cigarette but now the cigarette tastes rancid so I toss it out into the parking lot.

I'm not sure how long I can put up with this.

I've already kidnaped this man's daughter. I've extracted one of her teeth and am keeping her naked in a cage, feeding her garbage loaf. None of that feels good. Why don't I just buy a gun, follow Rumble and his friends until an opportunity arises, and take them all out?

Because I want this to be a lesson in vengeance. I'm not even sure I want to ultimately kill Rumble. Although I guess the alternative is to either kill his daughter or keep her prisoner for the rest of his life. I want him to have to live with that. I don't know how I can do that without hurting her. The notion of her falling in love with me is ludicrous but it makes me think of those messages I'd traded with her as Nila Townsend. I said whatever it was I thought Kasey wanted to hear, and while this was all fake and completely disingenuous, there was something about the pandering stereotypical hopefulness that was almost refreshing. Why do I always equate hope with ignorance? Am I cynical? Have I just never seen anything work out for anybody? Has it worked out fine for them, but their definition of happiness is less than or different than mine? Is it because I think wanting to be happy means mocking all the suffering of the world? But what have I ever done to ease any of that suffering? Doing what I'm now doing isn't easing anyone's suffering but my own and I'm not even so sure about that.

Another song stops and a new one starts. This one makes me think of a perverted late night office party where everyone is trying way too hard to have too much fun.

I light another cigarette and think about skipping to the next song but, I don't know, this one's growing on me.

There's a tap on my window and I nearly jump out of my skin, dropping my cigarette. I search the passenger seat floorboard until I spot the glowing cherry and pluck it up. Once retrieved, I turn my attention to the person who tapped on my window, fully expecting to see either Rumble or a cop.

It's neither.

It's a very cute girl—dark hair, dark skin—who looks no older than seventeen. Doesn't seem very threatening. I lower my window.

"Yeah?" I say.

"Hey," she says.

"Hey."

"Whatcha doin?"

I look toward the club and say, "Where did you come from?"

The girl smiles and it's a beautiful thing.

"Sorry if I scared you," she says. "I live back there." She points behind my car and I vaguely recall an apartment complex back there.

"And . . . can I help you?"

She smiles again and it really is a beautiful thing. Unruined. She must be young.

"Can I bum a smoke?"

I shake one from the pack and hand it to her.

"Gotta light?" she asks.

I spark my lighter and hold it out to her. She touches the end of the cigarette to the flame, takes a deep drag, and exhales. She's leaning against the car with her hand on the roof and staring at the back of the club.

"Thanks," she says. "Anything I can help *you* with?"

"No," I say. "I was just . . ." I can't tell her what I'm really doing.

"Workin up the nerve to go in?"

"Actually just getting ready to leave." But if she's been watching my car from her apartment, she knows exactly how long I've been sitting here.

She backs away from the car and bends over so her face is once again at my level and I'm expecting her to call me out.

Instead she says, "I hope you got what you came for," and looks at my crotch.

"I'm . . . uh, I'm good."

She takes another drag from her cigarette and blows it into the car.

"I bet for what you spent in there I could've gave you a real good time."

I'm pretty slow and not used to these things so it takes me up until this point to realize what's happening.

"I'm not really looking for that type of thing."

She laughs. "Then I guess you just came here for the overpriced drinks, huh?"

I don't have an answer for her so I decide to change subjects completely.

"What's your name?"

"What do you want it to be?"

I shrug and say, "Clyde, I guess."

She wrinkles her face.

"How old are you, Clyde?"

"How old you want me to be?"

I roll my eyes.

"How do you know I'm not a cop, Clyde?"

"Cause there's one parked out front."

"And what if he pulls around back here?"

"He ain't gonna do that."

"And how do you know that?"

"He's with one of my friends for the next few minutes."

"Bad cop," I say.

"Party cop," she says. "I can make you feel real good, hon."

"Get in the car," I say.

She comes around to the passenger side and hops in and I'm overwhelmed by her smell and her shorts are so tiny she seems to fill the passenger seat with nothing but sinewy brown thighs.

"Only thing I do in cars is BJs and handies. You want anything else you gotta take me to a hotel. You gotta treat me nice."

She's suddenly very professional and not as young as I thought she was and I'm telling myself I wasn't going to do anything with her anyway but now, with all the uncertainty shattered, I'm not even curious.

I pull my wallet out of my pocket, extract two twenties, and hold them out to her. She hesitates taking them and I know why. She wants me to place it on one of those glorious thighs or tuck it into the pocket of those tight shorts or slip it into the neckband of her low-cut tank top because she knows men and she knows once they have that taste, they can't say no. But I keep it there in between her and me, in the haze of her intoxicating scent, pinched between my thumb and middle finger.

"This is gonna floor you," I say, "but I don't want that kind of thing."

She takes the final drag from her cigarette and flings it out the window, offering me what I suppose is her "I don't fuck around" face.

"I don't do nothin too weird," she says. "Word gets out you do weird shit and that's all you end up doing. I do *not* want to be known as the girl who does weird shit."

"Just take the money. What I want has nothing to do with either of our bodies."

She takes the money and it disappears so fast I don't even see where it goes.

"You ever seen that black van before?"

And I know by the way she's backing away from me that I've already lost her. I should have taken her to a cheap motel, stripped her down, and tied her up before I started asking these kinds of questions.

"I think if you're asking that you already have a real good idea of the answer." She's already opening the door, her back turned to me, leaving me to stare at the band of orange underwear visible above the waist of her shorts.

Before slamming the door, she says, "This is the worst music I've ever heard in my life. My pussy dried up the second I got in your car. Just FYI."

And I'm left speechless, the girl nowhere in sight, staring at that black van like it's a mobile abyss.

Also, it's entirely possible this music is really bad. I don't know. I haven't known anything for a while. It's that acceptance of uncertainty that's kept me alive this long.

I'm tired but I can't go to sleep. The adrenalized thrill of following Rudy Rumble has been supplanted by enervation at the sad reality of the girl's situation. I should have brought some coffee.

I turn off my music app and turn on the radio, hoping to find something more lively.

"If you're addicted to bowel movements—" I turn the station from the commercial I've already heard a hundred times until I find some driving classic rock I've probably heard a thousand times or more. I'm so bored by it I keep going until I find some energetic dance music I've never heard before and wouldn't seek out in a million years. Whatever it takes to keep me awake.

I had been curious about that bowel movement commercial the first time I'd heard it. A co-worker explained to me that it was a natural progression of opiate addiction. Apparently those people never shit so when they get clean, they become addicted to the shitting, some of them going so far as to get hooked on enemas and laxatives. Seems like a more natural high to me.

I take a drink of water and place the bottle to my forehead. I light another cigarette.

This music now playing makes me feel young and gay and also slightly angry but I am okay with all of that.

I've been sitting out here for nearly an hour.

Patience, I tell myself. This is all going to take patience. I can't rush anything.

Why not?

Why drag it out?

Rudy Rumble either lives knowing his daughter is safe and alive or not knowing where she is. I can draw it out for as long as possible but that only makes things more excruciating for Kasey and me.

Unless I'm enjoying what I'm doing to her.

The song fades and the DJ tells me I'm listening to Club 101 and they'll be right back with a half hour of continuous music after a short commercial break. It's a commercial for tooth extraction. "Healthy teeth! Rotten teeth! Weird teeth! We'll take em! We pay extra for gold and silver!" I take another drag from my cigarette and tongue a gap toward the back of my mouth. I wonder how much I could get for the rest of them. I wonder what they use them for. Then there's a commercial advertising jewelry made from prolapsed anuses and I don't really know what to think.

Eventually Rudy Rumble, Beach Boy, and the Cowboy all emerge from the back of Bedazzled, a short, thin blond girl in tow. The Cowboy yanks open the sliding door of the van and pulls at his crotch as the other three file in before him.

Then the screams start. Screams punctuated with laughter. But mostly screams.

There's a light on in the van but the windows are tinted so I can't see anything other than silhouettes. That's okay. I don't really want to know what's going on in there. I know there's a cop around front but have the suspicion he's probably well aware of what is happening in the van. I think about calling 911 but cell phones have rendered anonymity a thing of the past and the last thing I want to do is identify myself as being in this exact place at this exact time.

Still . . . it's tough to listen to.

The van moves periodically, rocking from side to side and bouncing up and down. Eventually the screams die down.

I smoke cigarette after cigarette.

The screams come back. These seem even more desperate than the ones from before. Then there is relative quiet followed by huge bursts of laughter and the side door of the van is once again slid open. The girl staggers out, completely naked. She's bloodied and bruised. Her hair looks wet and I think, *The weird shit.* She shakily walks around to the other side of the van before collapsing onto the pavement. Now the three men are behind her. The Cowboy's shirt is off and his sweaty torso glistens under the artificial light. He's cradling a bundle of something in his left arm. Beach Boy is totally naked save for the colostomy bag. Rudy Rumble wears what

I at first think is a mask before realizing it's the girl's underwear.

The Cowboy extracts something from the bundle he's holding and throws it at the girl. It hits her with a smack like wet cloth, which I'm pretty sure it is. He drills a few other pieces of clothes at her, the last one hitting her in the face and just kind of sticking there. Then Beach Boy moves over top of her and I know what's coming and when he finally squeezes the bag over her head, I can smell it from where I'm sitting and have to silence a gag.

Then they take turns kicking her on the ass hard enough for me to hear as she slowly pulls herself to the back of the club and they race back to their van, full of energy, and I think that must be the end of their night and they're driving out of the parking lot and I'm behind them at a casual distance and they're headed back downtown and a slight mist has started falling and it softens and spreads the city's glow and they pull into an alley beside a hotel and I wonder if they're all going to go in and get a room and fuck each other before they emerge from the van and begin unloading musical equipment.

I find a place to park on the street before giving it a few minutes and heading into the hotel.

As with many things in Dayton, the hotel looks like it was really nice somewhere around 1982. The lobby is dim—like every other light is blown—and smells like mildew and smoke. A youngish man with heavy, stoned eyes, wearing a polo shirt with 'Dayton Palace' on the left breast, approaches me. A scab oozes from the top of his left ear and he has a nervous cough.

"You here for the show?"

"Of course I'm here for the show." It's like three in the morning. I have no idea what the show is but can't think of any other reason to be here.

"Twenty bucks." He coughs and wipes the back of his hand across his lips.

Behind him, a light flickers and winks out above the front desk. He looks back over his shoulder and his eye twitches.

I pull my wallet out of my pocket and hand him a twenty-dollar bill.

"Don't make no trouble, okay? We don't like no trouble. Just everybody havin a real good time. Gettin real relaxed and havin fun."

I wonder if I look like a troublemaker or if he has to tell everyone this because everyone who lives here is a wild animal.

I think about telling him I'm going to fuck shit up, just to mess with him, but don't want to do anything to make me memorable.

"I'm just here for a good time, man," I say.

He grins a grin of rotten teeth and pats my upper arm. "We all like a good time."

I feel like if I don't move soon he'll just stand like this until somebody else comes through the door.

I sever contact with him and continue moving through the lobby, toward the sounds I hear on my left. I cast one more glance back at the clerk who is now staring at a light overhead. It, too, flickers out and he begins drifting back to the front desk.

Toward the back of the lobby, there's an opening for a bar. This is one of those hotels that has felt the need to name their bar and it's spelled out in a purple neon script above the entrance. Most of the neon is burned out but it looks like it's called Tropics.

It's surprisingly packed and much more brightly lighted than the lobby, which seems strange until I realize most of the light is coming from panels behind the stage and I figure, at one time, they were probably not all white. It's as bright as a summer day and the effect is oddly disorienting. That wall, that's probably the owner's pride and joy.

The whole place is filled with fake palm trees, some of them inflatable, and a cloud of smoke hangs in the air. To the right of the entrance is a faux tiki bar with a cardboard sign reading: "Plastic Cups 2$." I'm guessing this is because it's illegal to sell alcohol after 2:30, but maybe it's okay to sell cups full of free alcohol? I don't know. The logic sounds shaky but maybe they think they've found some magic loophole. The idea of a place like this actually having a liquor license to lose is moderately terrifying.

To try not to stick out too much I move next to another lone bearded man who's talking into his phone with creased brows.

"Look, dude, my building has a pool, so bring your trunks. I don't care if a Speedo is all you have. That's all I have too. That's all anybody has. It'll be just us guys. No girls. We'll hit the pool and then throw some shit on the grill."

His brow straightens back out and a look of near ecstasy washes over his face.

"Right on. Right on. Awesome. I'll see you guys there."

The eyebrow crease returns as the person on the other end of the line says something.

"Yeah, man. I've been meaning to get it trimmed for a while. I've got an appointment tomorrow. I'm not going to embarrass myself. Come on."

Maybe he's talking about his beard, which is anomalously unkempt given the rest of his stylish appearance.

"See ya, bro." He brings the phone away from his ear and taps the screen.

Without even glancing at me, he pushes his way through the crowd and to the front of the stage where he raises both fists into the air and I can't figure out if it's a pose of defiance or aggressive anticipation.

The wall of lights behind the stage change to pink and then lavender. Rudy Rumble, Beach Boy, and the Cowboy emerge from stage right to wild applause. They've changed into sweaters and khaki pants and go about plugging in their instruments. Rudy Rumble is center stage with a triangle-shaped keytar. The Beach Boy has an electric clarinet at stage left and the Cowboy is stage right, towering over a keyboard.

They start playing the blandest music I've ever heard at an incredibly uncomfortable volume.

After a few minutes, no one is really paying any attention.

Rudy Rumble says into the microphone, "We're Double-R and The Fiber-Optics," and there's a smattering of applause before they launch into their next horrendous song. I'm pretty sure the Cowboy is just hitting a key on the keyboard and they are all just striking poses with the instruments and getting sweaty.

It's quite possible I'm filled with resentment for Rudy Rumble.

Here's a man roughly my age who's doing exactly what he wants to do with absolutely no repercussions, either from the outside or self-inflicted. His daughter has been missing for days and he seems unconcerned. He's involved in some really bad, really dark shit, but doesn't feel the need to remain off the radar. And, looking at him up there on stage, he is having *fun*. His friends are too. They've been having fun all evening. It's like this sad Midwestern world was made for them. It's like they're feeding off it. Like it's their playground. There's almost something zen about it. I've managed to keep myself relatively content, but I probably haven't had fun since I was eighteen or nineteen. Whatever fun I may have had was tempered by the dread of having to do shit I really didn't want to do just so I could keep myself alive.

This was a really bad idea.

I walk out of Tropics behind a couple and their pit bull. The man has the leash in his right hand and is using his left to support the woman.

"You puke, I can't catch it this time," he says. "Hands are full."

She slurs something and leans harder on him. They're moving really slow but I don't want to go around them because I find the dog intimidating.

Luckily we're almost to the edge of the lobby where the hallway ends and I can give them a wide berth. This turns out to be a good thing. As they reach the edge of the lobby the woman slides down off the man, onto her hands and knees, and vomits onto the floor.

"Jesus fucking Christ," the guy says.

The dog is immediately lapping up the puke and licking the strings of bile hanging from the woman's face and she's loving it, her head thrown back, laughing as the man stands by, looking exhausted, like he has no control over anything and I get the feeling, and the clerk is now approaching them.

"You don't get that dog outta here, I'm gonna fuck it. You hear?"

I'm now nearly at the front door and I hear the man say, "This dog's doin you a favor."

"Yeah. I'll fuck that dog in its little doggy asshole and clean the floor with your fucking face." It doesn't even sound threatening, just like something he has to say. He's not even raising his voice.

At the door, I turn and look back. They're not even close to each other, just standing there exchanging lazy insults like they're both too tired or high to really do anything about it.

The driver's side mirror of my car is smashed and someone has placed a glossy postcard advertising a strip club under my wiper. I remove it and throw it on the street, get in my car, and drive to an all-night porn store nearly an hour away where I buy five large dildos.

It's nearly dawn by the time I get back home and I sit on the back porch and smoke a couple of cigarettes and try to unwind as the neon of the city dies in the rising light and the world comes alive around me.

That's when it loses focus.

SCORING DRUGS THE LAZY WAY

The idea of trying to score heroin makes me nervous but I need to make sure Kasey is hooked on something. That's just the way it has to be. I've been reasonably healthy my entire life and only go to the doctor every couple of years for a routine physical, mainly to make sure I don't have prostate cancer, an unavoidable reaper's blade to most men in my family. Getting cancer is the only thing we've consistently done well. To my dismay, everything always comes back fine. My doctor, an obese Pakistani man, always laughs and tells me I will probably live forever. I usually feel powerful when I leave. From everything I've heard, however, opioids are given out like candy around here. So I just need to find someone who can get me some opioids, the cheaper alternative to making an appointment and pretending to have some kind of made-up pain. I don't even know the names of opioids so I have to go online and do some research so I know what to look for when I go through Lisa's medicine cabinet.

When I get there, Austin is napping. I excuse myself to go to the bathroom so I can survey the situation. She has a couple of things. Something called Opana and, the big one, OxyContin. I'll have to come back for it, but it looks like the yield will be around thirteen pills. Probably not enough. The more shocking find is the amount of antidepressants and I wonder how depressed my sister actually is. Then I think of her life and her husband and how well she manages to cope and it all makes some kind of sense. She's just stoned out of her head the entire time. Surprisingly, there isn't one container with Harold's name on it.

We waste an hour or so drinking her cheap coffee. I have to really suck it down so it'll make unquestionable sense when I have to once again visit the bathroom before I leave. By the time Austin wakes up I'm so caffeinated I feel out of my head and I frantically play with him—tickling him and dangerously tossing him up in the air and feeding him with a really shaky hand—and I know he is in no way prepared for the horrors of life awaiting him. Preparing him would be a risky business though, because he's just as likely to become a monster like Rudy Rumble.

I again excuse myself to the bathroom before leaving. I empty the necessary pill bottles into my pockets, hug Austin close to me, and head back to the neighborhood, back to the girl in the cage.

I pass Kim Barrel on my way. She's standing in her front yard with two of her dogs on leashes. She's completely topless and her breasts are the size and texture of two large cantaloupes. I think about calling social services or something when I get into the house and then think maybe she's just having a bad day. It isn't until I'm lying in bed that night, trying to erase the screaming from my brain, that I have two thoughts about Kim Barrel:

1. She probably has a lot of opioids. Having to walk around supporting breasts like that, not to mention being pretty obese otherwise, has probably twisted her spine to the point where it resembles a San Francisco street.

2. She has a key to my house.

This last thought fills me with so much panic I have to talk myself out of going over there immediately after having it.

MEDITATION

Kasey sits calmly in the cage and I think it must just be the first dose of opioids I administered yesterday. She's covered in bruises and her eyes are closed. I stand a couple feet from the cage, watching her.

"I know you're there," she says, startling me.

"I brought your ga—, your food."

"I don't need it."

"So, what? You're going to hunger strike now?"

"I'm just not hungry. And it tastes really bad. What is it?"

The last thing I want is for her to engage me in conversation. It's hard enough to divorce her from the girl I met on Facebook, the vulnerable girl in a moderately abusive relationship I managed to exploit. It's hard to see her as the daughter of a monster. It's hard not to see her as a daughter. It's hard not to see her as Ally.

"It's food. I'm just going to leave it here in case you decide to eat."

I place the pinkish brown slab on the floor.

Her calmness unnerves me. I know if I walk away without breaking that layer of iciness I'm going to feel like she's won this round. That's how I see it. Like some kind of prizefight, only I haven't figured out what the prize is yet. I get the staple gun and spend the next ten minutes in a blind rage.

A PERFECT DREAM

I have a dream where I'm driving a huge van. The most unfamiliar music I've ever heard is coming through the speakers. It's radiating more of a feel than an actual sound and that feeling is light and warm and starts somewhere in my gut, spreading out to all my extremities. Ann and Ally and Austin are all in the van. They're in the back, which seems cavernous, no seats, and they're all laughing and looking out the windows, ooh-ing and aah-ing at the sights. I'm on the highway surrounding Dayton but it seems exceptionally elevated, like we're in the clouds. Tall buildings ascend from the clouds and these are not typical Dayton buildings. They are tall skyscrapers that look scrubbed and new, foreign to the point of bordering on fantastical.

"Is that where they make the dreams," Austin says and it doesn't even strike me as odd that this is the first time I've ever heard him say words.

"Yeah, baby," Ally says, "that's where the dreams are made."

When I wake up I feel good but then I get immediately sad because I know it was all a dream and I wanted to live there forever.

THE HOUSE THAT SCREAMS TOO MUCH

My knocking sends Kim Barrel's dogs into a yapping frenzy. It takes a while before I hear her harshly yelling at the dogs to shut the fuck up. She opens the door, the dogs leaping up around her, gnashing their teeth at imaginary things in the air.

"Hey, Kim," I say.

She stares blankly at me.

"Remember when I gave that key to you a while ago? I need it back."

She rubs her mottled forehead with her right hand, cups the left under a breast and jiggles it, like her memory resides in a mammary gland or something. Thankfully, she's wearing a shirt today.

"I ain't got nothin to give you," she says.

"I'm just . . . I'm asking for my key back."

"I didn't take your fuckin key!" she barks.

I think about taking the hammer I have in my pocket, bashing her in the head with it, and forcing my way into her house where I will take my key back and all of her opioids and then I could feel better about what I'm doing to Kasey because she won't feel so singled out and alone because this is just what I do, this is just who I am—a serial assaulter of women.

Instead I say, "I brought Hamm's," and motion down to the thirty-pack on the stoop.

She has to step back to see it because her breasts and belly are so big. She cocks her head to the side and licks her lips.

I bend down and hoist it up.

"How bout we get this thing in your fridge?"

"You ain't gonna rape me, are you?"

"Absolutely not."

"And you ain't gonna drink all my Hamm's?" Now she laughs, revealing the nominal teeth in her mouth and I see a dim spark of the Kim Barrel I know.

"I don't drink," I say. "It makes me crazy. This is all for you. As thanks for keeping an eye on that key."

I transfer the pack of Hamm's to under my arm and pull the screen door back. It makes a squealing sound and falls completely out of the frame. Two small dogs dart between my legs and out into the yard.

Kim Barrel doesn't seem to notice any of this. She's focused intently on the beer.

Her house is, as expected, completely filthy, with a thick scent that feels like a living thing. I shuffle through the trash on my way to the kitchen.

"Where's the fridge?" I call.

"Ain't got one," she says. "Just put it on the floor."

I set the beer on the floor, on top of what might be a cat carcass stuck to a pizza box from a local place that hasn't been in business for the last three years.

"And bring me one!" she calls. "I'm ready to get comfy!"

I rip open the paperboard and grab a can, my mouth watering only slightly.

When I get back into the living room, Kim Barrel has taken off all her clothes.

The worst thing I can do is point this out to her.

"Do you mind if I use your restroom?" I ask. "Maybe you can find that key?"

"Keys! Keys! Keys!" she shrieks. "All these bitches want my keys!"

Because of the current situation, I strive extra hard to maintain eye contact.

I turn to go toward the bathroom but the path looks nearly insurmountable. Then I think it's only normal people who keep pills in the medicine cabinet. Someone like Kim Barrel, she's just going to put them wherever she wants.

She pounds her Hamm's, crushes the can, and throws it on the floor.

"Looks like you're a thirsty girl. You need another one."

I head back into the kitchen, scanning for pill bottles. I see a few near the sink. I imagine Kim Barrel tossing back fistfuls of pills before sticking her head under the faucet and chugging water. Fuck. She probably doesn't even need water. Probably just washes them down with Hamm's. A couple of the bottles are painkillers, surprisingly full, and I don't fool around with emptying them out. I just put them in my pockets, figuring Kim Barrel will not hear them rattling around because those little dogs have not shut up since I got here and I imagine the house filled with dogs, barking and yapping from the attic and basement, behind the couple closed doors I can see, and I don't feel guilty for taking painkillers she might need because I brought her Hamm's and that's probably just as good.

I go back into the living room and hand her a fresh Hamm's.

"Hey, you know, I can probably just grab that key," I say.

"You ain't gonna get off my back about that fuckin key, are you?"

She wobbles over to a bloated and slouching entertainment center and wraps a meaty hand around a Yuban coffee can. She turns the can upside down and at least two dozen keys hit the layers of debris covering the floor.

"I guess I'm just giving away houses now. I own all these."

I'm as confused by the sheer amount of keys she has as by her line of reasoning. I look at the scattered mess of keys and think I probably should have put some sort of ornamentation on mine.

"I'm thinkin I got one I gotta sell though. It screams too much."

A chill races down my spine.

I take my chances and pluck up the newest looking one.

"Let me see." She squints her eyes. A trail of beer runs from one corner of her mouth.

I hold the key out to her.

"Yep," she says. "That's the one. You want it, you got it."

I think about asking her what she meant when she said the house screams too much but think I probably don't want to know the answer. I just want to get out of here.

NO HISTORY

I check the *Dayton Daily News* website every day, looking for any sign that Kasey's disappearance has been reported. It's been over a week and I still haven't seen anything. The only reason I can see for them to not report it is that they know she's been kidnaped and they probably have a really good idea of who did it.

I convince myself I'm just being paranoid before thinking about what Kim Barrel said. I know there is no way she heard the screams from outside the house. Meaning she has to have been in the house while I wasn't here. Couple that with the fact she was the person who babysat Austin the night I did the deed and Kim Barrel could be a valuable resource to the police.

Had she come into the house when I wasn't here?

There's no other way she could have heard the screams.

But she's crazy so it's entirely possible the screams were coming from her head.

Also, she's so obviously crazy I can't imagine her ever being seen as a reliable source.

There's probably no one on this street who could be seen as a reliable source.

This is what I use to dissolve my paranoia. There is absolutely no reason why someone like me should have a girl in a cage in his basement. It wouldn't make any sense. I'm not a sociopath. I'm not a serial killer. I've never done anything like this before. There is no history. No pattern.

DEATH AND MORE CUM

At Handstands again. Rudy Rumble has assembled a good coterie. The Cowboy is there. There are two guys, nearly identical, who I think of as the Hunters. They both have short gray hair, the style probably acquired from Supercuts or some barbershop with a sports theme. They're each wearing razor shades, camouflage hoodies, and dad blue jeans. They both have the same doughy physique best summed up by the phrase "gone to seed." There are a number of people of the same vaguely generic ilk—blue-collar types who aren't poor but have never taken the time or interest in cultivating any sense of personal style or aesthetics. In short, what we used to call Boring Old Fucks. I should know. I'm one of them.

The Beach Boy is not there.

I try to sit close enough to hear what they're saying without being noticed. I pretend to be absorbed in the book on my phone.

Rumble seems genuinely distraught, pounding the Bud Lights and looking earnestly at his boring old fuck friends as they approach him and clap him on the back and engage him in a handshake that ends in a hug and I have a moment of panic when I think this is about Kasey and maybe these people are some kind of assembled search party or lynch mob. Only panic isn't exactly the correct word because I feel like that is exactly what should be happening. That it should have been happening the day after her disappearance. At least after he'd received the tooth.

A man wearing an orange and black Cincinnati Bengals sweatsuit claps Rumble on the back and says, "We're all gonna miss ole

Donny."

Rumble blinks away tears and says, "Thanks, man. He taught me everything I know."

"I know you two went back a ways."

Donny. Are they talking about the Beach Boy? He isn't here and his health certainly seemed to be on the decline the last time I saw him.

Since my phone's already right there in front of me, I go to the *Dayton Daily News* website. I know their obituary section well. Turns out I don't have to go that far. One of the dropdown headlines is:

City Mourns Loss of Former County Commissioner Donald O'Malley

The article goes on to list all of his accomplishments along with his surviving family members. It doesn't detail his penchant for emptying his colostomy bag in parking lots and onto young girls. Turns out I wasn't too far off with the Beach Boy moniker. The article details O'Malley's love for all things nautical so I'm unsurprised when I learn that the funeral will be in New Smyrna Beach, Florida, and O'Malley's ashes will be loaded aboard his yacht, Pearl Schaft, before being scattered in the Atlantic. I find it vaguely satisfying his incinerated body will be trickling down into the cold depths of the ocean, becoming part of its floor, millions of sea creatures dropping their shit onto him for years to come.

Another man is talking to Rumble.

"You goin to the funeral?"

And I'm sure he'll say no because he has things to tend to here on the home front, like the mysterious disappearance of his daughter, but he says, "Flyin down tomorrow. His family's not takin it too well."

"I'm not gonna be able to make it but make sure to give em my regards."

"Will do. Will do."

I continue sitting there, listening to this outpouring of support and emotion, while pretending to scroll through my phone.

At one point, someone claps me on the back and says, "Cheer up, Mr. Broody!"

I turn and look up to see the Cowboy towering behind me.

I don't know what to do, so I force a smile and raise my glass.

He hoists his with his right, points to me with his left, and says, "That's right! This is Handstands—a real fun place! Says it right there on the window."

I think his current line of banter might be a little tone deaf given why they all seem to be gathered here, but then I realize the whole tone of the group has shifted. They probably got here too early, drank a little too hard to combat the natural sadness, and have now gone straight to an aggressive need for excitement.

The Cowboy puts his glass down on the table and says, "Don't I know you?"

"I . . . don't think so."

"What's your name?"

I don't expect this and know I take too long to respond. I glance down at the Haruki Murakami book on my phone and say, "Harry . . . Harry Markum."

"Mar-kum?" he says, distinctly enunciating each syllable.

"Yep."

"More come. That's what I'll call you. Ole Harry More Cum." And he smiles and looks really pleased with himself.

I don't know how to respond.

"Huh," he says, as though searching his memory. "I don't know anyone named Harry More Cum, pretty sure. I'm Lenny Thigpen. I own Lenny's Towing. Maybe I towed you somewhere along the line. If so, my apologies." He throws up a massive hand.

"Um . . . I don't think so. Nice to meet you." I try to turn my attention back to my phone and I can tell he's slightly offended. In a city like Dayton, you're sometimes treated like a celebrity if your name's all over the place. In fact, it's such a city of industry that it's probably the quickest way to celebrity.

"No, no," he says. "I get it. You want to play with your phone."

He's walking away and saying something about not understanding why people would come to a bar to play on their phone and I realize I've stayed way too long.

The guys have definitely drank way too much and now they're getting more emotional.

I've already paid for the one beer I've ordered all night. I haven't even taken a sip from it. I slip out of the bar as quietly as I can.

I make it through the party patio and wonder why my heart is racing. Sometimes I'm sensitive to my surroundings and other times I'm completely oblivious. My feet hit the pavement of the parking lot and I think maybe I'll be okay.

Then I hear laughter and the Cowboy saying, "Look at ole More Cum go."

Followed by a drunken chant of "More Cum go! More Cum go!"

And now my heart is really racing and the smart part of my brain says I should just put all pride aside and take off running for my car. They've all been drinking a lot and there's no way they could catch or follow me.

"Where ya goin, More Cum?" the Cowboy calls.

There's another part of me tenaciously clinging to what little shred of pride I have left.

I bridge this dichotomy the way I almost always do—by playing dumb. I pretend I don't hear them, continue my stalwart march to the car, hoping they'll be too drunk to bother.

I hear the Cowboy's boots behind me. Hear somebody else say "C'mon, Lenny. Leave it" and know it isn't Rudy Rumble because he wants to see what's going to happen.

A hand drops onto my shoulder and I stop and turn.

"Can I help you?" I say to a face that has become a mask. It's a look you see on a lot of mentally ill people around here—even the functional ones. The eyes and expression have turned inward, constantly scanning a secret map of desires and grievances. There is no communicating with someone wearing that mask. There is no convincing them. There is no arguing with them. Their script is already written.

"Where ya goin, More Cum?"

I should just smash my fist into that mask but my fists are small and I don't think it would have much effect.

"I'm going home." I don't make eye contact and continue moving toward my car.

He puts a big arm around my shoulder and I can smell the beer and the sweat hiding under an abundance of cologne.

"Well, let me help you get there. Where's your car?"

I point to my car. It's only a few steps away and my heart sinks when I realize how close I was. If I had just broken into a run, I would have made it without a problem and I never would have come back to Handstands and Rudy Rumble wouldn't see me again until the night I make him run his daughter over.

"You sure it's this one?"

"Pretty sure."

He looks exaggeratedly at my cheap little car and then down at me and says, "Yeah. Looks about right."

I take my keys out of my pocket and weasel out of his grip, think about driving a key into his eye.

"Guess I'll see you around," I say.

He takes a stronger grip on my shoulders, slamming me against the car. He slams me again and again until I lose my footing and fall to the ground.

That prideful part of me again rears its head. It says I should fight back but all logic tells me this would be a horrible idea. The Cowboy is about twice my size. Any fight I attempt is only going to stoke his inexplicable rage and anger even further.

He steps on my wrist holding the keys until I release them. He squats down and pistons a huge hand into my face. There's a bright white light and a flash of tremendous pain followed by a surprising but welcome numbness. I'm still fully conscious but play dead, hoping he doesn't keep going. He stands up and levels a couple of kicks at my ribs. He pauses like he's contemplating stopping before he grunts and goes back to kicking.

Now there's someone approaching him, saying "Lenny, man, c'mon. You don't want to kill him. Not here" and I again know it's not Rudy Rumble saying this.

There's a moment when I almost shit my pants because I imagine them loading me up into that van and taking me to a place where they can kill me or just beat and humiliate me as much as they want.

"This guy, man," the Cowboy says. "He don't like to have fun. And I bet he's a fucking liar."

"Let's just not do this tonight, okay?"

The Cowboy bends down and rolls me over. He reaches into my back pocket and pulls out my wallet.

"Take a picture of that," the Cowboy says and I assume he means my license.

I lie very still.

The wallet slaps the pavement next to me.

"Why did you lie to me?" the Cowboy says.

"C'mon, man. Leave it," the other man says.

"I don't like liars," the Cowboy says.

"Rudy's ready to go to Bedazzled. There's a girl there with a real long pussy. We need to get out of here."

The Cowboy grunts, picks up my keys, and hurls them. I don't even hear them come down so I imagine they completely cleared the parking lot.

He squats down again, one of his knees popping loudly, and says, "I know where you live."

And they're gone and I'm rolling over onto my side so the blood doesn't run down the back of my throat and I think about just lying there forever and about looking for my keys and end up calling Uber to come pick me up. I'll have to come back and look for my keys. I have no idea how I'm going to get into the house.

HUGS WITH TEETH

"You look worse than I do," Kasey says. She knows how bad she looks because I've placed a full-length mirror within view of the cage so I'm not the only witness to her decline.

Her voice snaps me back into the present. It's hard to focus. I've been standing there staring at her but not really seeing *her*. She's like a portal into some past life where things were better. Maybe they weren't even really better but they . . . what? Had more meaning? More purpose? But what's the point of purpose if it's just going to leave you and die?

"Can I . . . give you a hug?" I ask.

There's a sneer on Kasey's face and I hate it but what do I expect? That she likes any part of this?

"Why are you even bothering to ask?"

"Because . . . I don't want bars in the way. I want you to promise me you won't try to get away."

"Did my dad do that to you?"

Her question drives a nail into that ever-dying sliver of pride.

"No," I say. "It was the Cowboy."

"The Cowboy?"

He told me his name but it's not springing to the forefront of my thoughts.

"He, uh, runs a towing company. Big guy. Dresses like Johnny Cash."

"Oh, you mean Uncle Lenny."

"Yeah, him."

"You're in way over your head. These people are not like you."

"Am I, though? Are they even concerned with finding you?"

There's something in that that stings her a bit. The sneer has mostly dissolved and there's a steely hurt in her eyes, like she's purposefully hardening her expression so she doesn't cry.

"I lost my virginity to Lenny," she says. "I was thirteen. He's rich, you know? I thought we were going to get married. He was so nice to me. But afterward . . . he just told me he wanted to know what it was like."

"They're going to be out of town for the next couple of days. Funeral." I don't bother telling her whose. Maybe she'll think I killed the Cowboy. "Maybe I'll pay a visit to your mother."

"My mother's dead. The cunt who lives in that house is my stepmom."

"I'm sure he wouldn't want anything to happen to her."

The corner of her mouth turns up and she says, "Then you don't know her."

"How can I hurt him?" I ask.

"Let me out," she says.

"I can't do that."

"This is what he wants. *Exactly* what he wants. He doesn't care that I'm missing. I know that. I bet there hasn't even been anything about it in the news because he has the ability to suppress it."

"Why would he do that?"

"Because he needs to keep all of his secrets in the dark. The last thing he wants is for people to start asking questions."

"I can let you out to hold you, but that's it."

"I'd . . . I'd like that," she says and I have to try really hard to convince myself she actually means it.

I undo the padlock, now very aware of her complete nakedness. I've gotten so used to seeing it I've stopped thinking about it. I pull the door back and she just stands there. There's a moment where I contemplate entering the cage before realizing, if she does try to get away, she could potentially have the ability to lock me in the cage. That wouldn't turn out so well.

"Come on," I say. "I don't want anything more. I'm not going to do anything to you."

She slowly takes a couple of steps toward me and stands with her arms hanging limply by her sides. I step toward her, briefly repulsed by her stench. I wrap my arms around her shoulders, my hands ending up on her shoulder blades. Her skin is cool to the touch and almost sticky. I pull her into my warmth and think it must feel good to her. I'm trying not to cry, trying not to completely break down and tell her I don't want to be doing any of this, that I never wanted to hurt her.

She raises her head and lifts her small body up to her tiptoes and, at first, I have a crazy idea she's trying to kiss me before she's moving lightning fast, clamping her teeth onto my neck and it's so close to my ear I can hear my skin pop and the guttural growl coming from her throat. I hold her tighter, thinking I need to force her back into the cage. She drives a small but highly effective knee up between my legs and I hear her bare feet slapping across the painted cement floor. I fight the sick feeling in my lower stomach and dart after her but she's already at the top of the stairs and now I'm taking them two at a time, suddenly aware of how sore I am from last night's beating, and I think my balls might actually be swelling already and by the time I've made it through the kitchen and the living room she's already at the front door and when she throws it open and there's an explosion of bright daylight and I know for sure she's going to make it outside, there's a part of me that thinks I should just let her go, let her go and deal with the consequences or let her go and then eat all the remaining pills and put all of this behind me but I know I can't because I finally want something and it doesn't matter to me if that something is as petty or mean-spirited as justice or vengeance or whatever because it's the first thing I've wanted since my dreams for a happy family were shattered.

She reaches the yard and makes the mistake of pausing to decide which direction to bolt and scream for help. In the time it takes her to do that, I'm launching myself off the front stoop, and in a frankly surprising act of athleticism, I land close enough to clamp my hands around her narrow shoulders and drag her down onto the lawn. She's screaming but the only person outside is Kim Barrel, five houses away in a swirl of barking dogs and mental illness. I need to get Kasey back in the house before all the unemployed and elderly people can leave their houses to investigate the sounds.

I keep my arms wrapped around Kasey and stand up. She's kicking and screaming and this feels much worse, much more violent, than actually kidnaping her.

I get her back into the house and kick the door shut and I'm filled with red rage and don't know how I managed to feel any sympathy for this bitch, don't know how I managed to let her manipulate me, and I tell myself that no amount of pain I can inflict on her is too much, that she should heretofore be subject to the most brutal forms of torture I can think of.

I clamp my hand around the back of her neck and throw her down the basement stairs, her body smacking coldly onto the floor.

Some of the fight seems to have left her and I wonder if she feels the rage, knows that, for the first time since bringing her into my custody, I'm angry enough to kill her.

I hurry down the steps, grab her by the thin arms, and toss her into the cage like a bag of trash.

Then I clasp the lock shut with a sense of superiority, a sense of victory.

I say, "Worst hug ever," and go upstairs to inspect my neck wound in the bathroom mirror.

THERE IS NO HOPE
YOU ARE NOT A PART OF THIS WORLD
AND YOU MUST CREATE YOUR OWN REALITY

"I don't see it," I say from the passenger seat of Lisa's car. We're in the parking lot of Handstand's. Austin's sleeping in the back.

"What were you doing here anyway?"

I bite down my anger and decide to deliver the most Midwestern answer I can think of. "I was trying to have fun."

"Let me assure you that if you've started drinking again, it's not going to be much fun."

"What's that supposed to mean? I never really drank much. It's definitely not like I had a problem or anything."

"I just mean with our family history."

"You and Harold are too churchy."

"We don't even go to church."

"You know what I mean."

"No, I don't. Want to clarify?"

"Boring." I cut right to the chase, in no mood to deal with this today.

"Well," she chuffs, "maybe we'd be able to get out and really let loose if we weren't raising your grandson."

"You're not raising him. Just watching him most of the time." We both know this isn't really true.

"You're not going to find a decent woman in a bar. You're a fifty-year-old man. Why don't you use one of those online sites?"

"I'm tired of having this conversation with you. There are other things to do in bars besides drink and troll for women."

"Like what?"

"There's food and . . . people and . . . sports."

"So you're into people and sports now?"

"Oh yeah," I say.

"So what is it about your newfound enthusiasm for people and sports that would prevent you from driving your car home last night?"

I've already had to answer Lisa's battery of questions regarding my appearance—the black eyes, the patch on my neck—and feel like just confirming what she wants to hear—that I'm becoming a lousy drunk—is ultimately less humiliating than telling her I was beaten up in the parking lot and the bully took my keys and threw them far away.

"I never said I *didn't* drink."

She shakes her head and says, "Something's going on with you. I hope you're not in trouble."

"I'm gonna go find out where the hell my car is."

Up by the entrance to Handstands, there's a metal sign proudly announcing that the parking lot is owned and maintained by Rumble-thon LLC and that all towing is executed by Lenny's Towing and Wrecking. What a cute couple. I call the phone number and give them my license plate number and they confirm my car is there. It's in a really bad part of town and I know Lisa's going to balk at having to take me there. I go search the banks of grass at the edge of the parking lot, hoping to see my keys. Luckily I have spares of everything because I don't see them.

I take a deep breath before walking back to the car and Lisa. Every time I'm around her, I'm reminded of what it was like growing up with her. Only with many years of perspective have I been able to put it into context. It's like if you feel like you've just met the dumbest person ever—like, the person who, after thirty seconds of talking them, you want to walk away because it's the most obvious, juvenile, attention-grabbing shit you can think of—and then you're like, yeah, that's my life, that's what I'm living in. It's kind of like that. Like when you saw the trailer for that movie and thought, "That looks like the worst thing ever," and then it's the top-grossing box office hit that weekend and then, dear fucking god, it wins tons of awards and you suddenly realize there's no hope, you're not a part of this world, and you can't help but to further create your own reality.

I think about telling her this and decide I shouldn't. She's not really the problem anyway. The problem was getting out of our parents' house and realizing the vast majority of the world is just like her. Meaning I'm the problem.

When I get back in the car, I have a brief, heart-stopping moment where I realize that now, not only do Rumble and Lenny have my name and address, they might also have keys to my house and car and I'm actually a little surprised when I get home around two hours later and Kasey's still there, nearly comatose in the cage. I felt bad for being so rough with her that I gave her a much larger dose of opiates than previously. They seem to be having the desired effect.

BIG CIGARETTE

There's a loud knock on the door. I'm in the bathroom shaving my head and face with electric clippers and think about ignoring it until I remember the Cowboy has my name and address and I should probably at least make sure it isn't him so my anxiety doesn't ramp up to an unmanageable level. I glance at the mirror. My head is only half shaved and a lot of the longer hairs are clinging to the stubble where my beard used to be. I look like an escaped mental patient. I brush some of the hair away and give my hands a quick dusting and cross the living room to the front door.

Through the peephole, I see a blond guy who could be a rough-looking teenager or a young-looking middle-aged man standing on the stoop. His unkempt hair and pajama pants make him look like he just rolled out of bed. He isn't wearing anything besides the pajama pants. He probably isn't hiding a gun or anything but I still don't want to open the door because I don't want to talk to anybody.

He knocks again.

"Can I help you?!" I shout through the door. If he's from the neighborhood, he's used to people not being too friendly.

"You got a cigarette?"

I'm slightly stunned by the question. This is the first time I've been panhandled in my house.

"I don't smoke," I say.

"Good luck with that," he says before turning and walking across the street to the next house and I think, *Smartass*.

I finish grooming and inspect myself in the mirror. The swelling in my nose is almost completely gone. It now has a bend it didn't have before. Surprisingly, there is almost no sign of the bite wound on my neck. The black eyes have faded to interesting shades of purple and yellow and red more alarming than the original dark storm clouds. The lack of anything other than a sparse crop of hair on my head makes the injuries all that more apparent and I think cutting everything off was probably a bad idea. I'm planning a return trip to Bedazzled tonight and, while I'm pretty sure Rumble is not going to be there, I still want to make myself as unrecognizable as possible.

I strip down to take a quick shower to get all the clippings off. Otherwise, I'll be itchy the rest of the day.

After drying off and putting on some clean clothes, there's another knock on the door. It's the same guy as before. I open the door in a quick burst of anger.

"I told you, man, I don't have any cigarettes."

He shakes his head and holds up his right hand. "Don't need one," he says.

In his hand he holds possibly the fattest cigarette I've ever seen, like he's taken four rolling papers and glued them together.

"I was wondering if you had a way of lighting this," he says.

I briefly consider walking him to the backyard and building a fire so he can light his monster cigarette but my anger has subsided somewhat so I say, "Hang on," and go grab my lighter and cigarettes from the kitchen.

By the time I get back to the living room, he's standing just inside the front door.

I have a momentary twinge of panic before telling myself he's probably just out of his head and ultimately harmless.

I step around him, open the front door, and jerk my head for him to follow me. He snaps out of his daze and steps out onto the stoop with me. I hand him the lighter and sit down on the steps. He sits down beside me and spends a few seconds lighting his cigarette and coughing before handing my lighter back to me.

It's bright and hot in the early afternoon.

I take a cigarette from my pack and light it.

"I thought you said you don't have any cigarettes," he says.

"I said I don't smoke."

"But you're smoking."

"I wasn't when you asked. I'd quit."

"Nobody wants to share their cigarettes around here. Everyone's a demon protecting their own little piece of hell. They want to keep all the smoke to themselves."

"Sounds about right."

"Your house is real nice."

"Thanks. You live around here?"

"I just moved in with that Ken guy. You ever met him? He said I could live there if I mowed the grass for him. His house ain't so nice, though. Only got one window and no electricity or running water. The window don't even got glass." He takes a drag of his cigarette and sighs out some smoke. "I've been shitting in the backyard."

"I haven't had the chance to meet him yet. I mostly keep to myself."

"Most of the people around here are assholes anyway."

I have to smile at that. It doesn't take people long to figure it out.

The guy scuffs the soles of his bare feet along the cement. I don't know his name and don't really care because it would mean introducing myself and I usually wait for other people to do that first.

"You ever hear of a guy named Rudy Rumble?" I ask.

He suddenly raises his arms above his head like he's at a party or a sporting event or something and says, "Double-R, the Parking Lot King! Hell yeah, I've heard of him. Dude's a fucking saint."

He lowers his arms and takes a big hit of his big cigarette.

I take a drag and think about what to say. I'd only ever talked about him to Ally during one of her brief bouts of sobriety and that was only toward the end. I find myself hesitant to talk about Rumble, like anything I say can potentially lead him back to me, especially now that he has so much of my information. What if word gets back to him that *that guy* is now asking questions about him?

"Really?" I say. "I thought he was like a big-time drug dealer or something."

"More like a doctor giving us the medicine we need. A drug *provider*."

"Hm. Guess I never really thought of it like that."

"It's not like everybody thinks, you know."

"No?"

68

He violently shakes his head and says, "No, no, man. Ain't nothing like any of that. He's different."

"How so?"

"We ain't really supposed to talk about it."

"I mean . . . if he's doing good work . . . sounds like you'd want to spread the gospel, you know?"

He shrugs and says, "So, what? You looking to score?"

I think about that and say, "What if I was?"

"Sorry, man, I ain't got any. You'd have to go to the show."

"The show?"

He kind of rolls his eyes and slumps his shoulders and says, "Jesus, man, how long you lived here? You don't know about the show?"

I throw my hands up and say, "Guess not. I told you I don't really leave the house much."

"Well, okay, man. It moves around from parking lot to parking lot."

"What goes on there?"

"I'm not really supposed to talk about it. Everybody's welcome though. They have em every month. Let me just say, if you're looking to score, you won't be disappointed. Nothin like a buncha people comin together, gettin real relaxed, and havin a good time. No harm in that. Next one's comin up in about a week. It's gonna be in the parking lot where K-mart used to be."

"On, uh, Woodman?"

"That's the one."

"Maybe I'll check it out."

"Ain't got nothin to lose. Don't cost nothin."

"And I'll get some . . . some stuff just for showing up?"

"Oh yeah." He takes a drag and there's something like yearning in his eyes. "You just gotta check it out, man. It don't make no sense if I try to tell you about it."

"So he just . . . gives the stuff away?" I'm still trying to wrap my head around it.

"Well, probly not all the time. But at the shows, sure."

"How can he do that?"

"Rumor has it he and his boys go out to, uh, places like Columbus and Cincinnati and Youngstown and shit and they find the *real* drug dealers. You know, like the real bad men from Mexico, and they . . . take the law into their own hands. They take what they want." Here he drops his voice to a conspiratorial whisper, leans into me, and says, "Rumor has it Double-R has a whole barn outside Xenia where he keeps these bad guys. Like his own fuckin prison. Friend of mine says if you go up there you can see em out workin the fields. He keeps these, like, shock collars on em to keep em from gettin away." He laughs. "I'd love to go up there and take a look at it."

I want to tell him it sounds sick but what do I know? I have a girl in a cage in my basement.

I can't tell if this guy's telling the truth or if he's just a delusional lunatic or a combination of the two. Either way, I doubt I'm getting much more out of him. I stub my cigarette out on the stoop, stand up, and say, "See you around," before heading back into the house.

He nods his head and takes another drag from his cigarette. The hand holding the cigarette is stained yellow-brown. I continue watching him from inside the house. After finishing his cigarette, he sits there for another minute or two before standing and wandering to the edge of my lawn where he bends over and throws up.

I sit on the couch and think about what he's told me, imagining it mostly as just a partial truth, a junkie justifying his own actions while exonerating the man who supplies him.

CLYDE

I'm in my car in the back parking lot of Bedazzled listening to something called "Vaporwave Night" on satellite radio and smoking cigarettes. I'm waiting for Clyde, but I don't know if she's going to show up. It's not as late as it was the other night so I might be waiting a while. The music is extremely relaxing and I'm afraid I might fall asleep. It doesn't help that I broke one of Kasey's pills in half and took it to help calm my nerves. I've never actively solicited a prostitute before and don't want to chicken out.

Shortly after parking here, a cop did a sweep of the parking lot and now I'm growing slightly paranoid that if I'm still sitting in my car when he makes another sweep he's going to approach me and ask some questions.

It's a nice night, warm and clear. I decide to take a walk to try and perk myself up.

I get out of the car and stretch, looking at the apartment complex where Clyde said she lived. There are some nice well-lighted grounds surrounding the buildings and I feel like it should be okay to walk around there, not that this is a bad part of town anyway.

I climb the low grassy embankment separating the parking lot of Bedazzled from the apartment's grounds, find a concrete walkway, light a cigarette, and begin walking. There are a few people out walking their dogs but, other than that, it seems pretty quiet. Eventually I come to a group of three men standing around a grill. In the low artificial light, they all look the same. They're all wearing only Speedos, their well-muscled bodies on full display. They have the same short haircut and they all have well-groomed beards of about the same length. This feels oddly familiar. Have I dreamt something like this? They're listening to upbeat music, drinking beer from bottles, and seem to be having a pretty good time.

The path takes me around them, and as I'm passing, one of them turns to me and says, "Hey, guy, do you know how to grill corn?"

"Sorry, man," I say. "I've never grilled corn." But part of me wishes I had grilled corn. Part of me wishes I could just strip off my clothes and join their party or whatever it is, crawl out of the nightmare I'm in and show them how much of a wizard at grilling corn I am, but I'm way older than they are and my beard is gone and I don't even own a Speedo and, while I'm not fat, I have no muscles to speak of and I know there's no way I could fit in.

"I told you, bro," another man says. "Nobody grills corn."

A third man says, "Just look on your phone, dude. That'll tell you how. We've already been out here for like three hours."

"My phone's in my pants," the original guy says and they all explode with laughter.

For the first time, I notice a large plastic trash can overflowing with corn still in the husk and think, *They're never going to be able to eat all of that.*

By the time I get back to my car, Clyde is trolling the parking lot.

She doesn't see me right away so I make as much noise as possible getting into my car.

And like a predator scrounging for its prey, her head cocks slightly in the direction of my car, although she's trying to be discrete about it. I watch as she glides across the asphalt. I already have my window down, a cigarette at the ready.

"Hey, man," she says. "You got a—"

I hand her the cigarette.

She smiles. "Thanks. It's like you read my mind."

I'm assuming she doesn't remember me and probably wouldn't recognize me if she did.

I'm too impatient to sit through the whole routine again.

I light her cigarette and say, "I know what you do."

Her face cracks for just a second and I ease her fear by saying, "Don't worry. I'm not here to bust you."

She smiles and places her free hand to her chest and says, "Phew. Cause, you know, they never send the ones in uniforms to do that shit." Then I see a vague spark of recognition in her eyes and know she's good at what she does, with a bartender's uncanny ability to remember your name. "You were here the other night. Mr. Only Wants To Talk About People He Shouldn't Be Talkin About."

"Yeah." I light my own cigarette.

"Looks like you got the shit beat out of you."

"I had a board land on my face."

"Mean old board."

"Yeah. I was building a gazebo for my mom."

"Momma's boy, huh?"

"Moms, you know. We all got em."

"That's true. That's true." She takes a puff of her cigarette. "So you just come back to talk more? Don't look like your friends in the black van are here tonight."

"I don't think you'd be able to help me with what I need, unfortunately."

"Might surprise you."

"As I recall, you said you don't want to be the girl who does weird shit."

"Well . . . there's weird shit and then there's real weird shit."

"Look, I don't want to piss in your mouth or anything."

"What you got in mind?"

"Get in and I'll take you to a hotel. How many guys you been with today? Be honest. The more the better."

Her brows furrow in slight confusion. "About eight. Ten if you include my boyfriends." She pauses. "Oh wait, eleven if you count my stepbrother. I'm trainin him."

"Perfect," I say.

She smiles. "You ready to be number twelve?"

"We'll talk about it. Hop in."

I'm in the bathroom of the cheapest motel I've ever been in and find myself feeling really sad. I told Clyde to name her place, ready to cringe when she picked some place nice and expensive, and this was the first place she picked. This was her idea of a 'nice hotel' and it's probably because she doesn't even know nicer places exist. I try to relieve the sadness by convincing myself she's just thrifty and pragmatic, utilitarian, a good businessperson. This motel will get the job done just as easily as a more expensive one and maybe the amount the client saves on the room will be reflected on her tip.

We got into the room and I introduced her to the bag of dildos and explained to her what I wanted and she seemed really surprised when I told her I didn't even want to watch. She said if that was the case then this was going to be her easiest gig ever and seemed dubious. Then she pointed to the largest of the dildos and said, "I'll earn my money gettin that one in there."

After flushing my fourth cigarette down the toilet, there's a gentle tapping on the door.

"I'm done," she says.

I open the door. She's naked. I try not to look.

"You can put your clothes back on."

"For real?"

"Yeah. We're done here."

I turn my attention to the come-glazed dildos drying on the nightstand.

Clyde gathers up her clothes and starts putting them on.

"You really know how to make a girl feel like trash," she says.

"What do you mean?"

"This is my *job*. This is what I do. And you won't even look at me. It really does make me feel like you just rented my pussy. Not even *my* pussy. Just *a* pussy. Could have been anyone's. It's like going to McDonald's just to use the bathroom."

"I'm real sorry you feel that way."

"I don't think you're sorry at all."

"No. I am. Maybe. A little sorry, at least. I just don't . . . uh, I just don't do that anymore."

"Why? Your dick rot off?"

"It's just too morally and philosophically confusing. I'd rather not deal with the fallout."

"It's none of those things. It's a transaction. A transaction driven by *desire*. Nothing's easier than that."

"I just wouldn't feel good about myself."

She moves up behind me, wrapping her arms around my waist, taking my crotch in her hand, and whispering into my ear, "Sometimes it's *just* about feeling *good*, you know? I could make you feel real good."

There's a second where my cock twitches to life and I'm tempted.

"I haven't felt good in years." I pry her hand off me. "You want to put those things back in the bag?"

"Those things?"

"Yeah. Those . . ." and I wave my hand at the dildos.

She smiles and shakes her head. "My God, you can't even say it, can you?"

"Say what?"

"Dildo."

"Sure I can."

"Then tell me what you want me to do."

"Put the"—she leans toward me, waiting for me to say it—"*dildos* in the bag. There. Happy now?"

She squeals with delight and says, "You're a weird one."

"You hungry?"

"You buying?"

"Sure."

We go to Waffle House and I mostly phase out while she talks about herself and eats food that is eventually going to lead to obesity and diabetes and death and I drop her off in the parking lot of Bedazzled and give her way more money than I should.

It's really late by the time I get back home and Kasey's nearly comatose. She looks disgustedly at the bag of soiled dildos and I know she's not going to willingly do what I want her to so I have to use nailstick to get her to cooperate. By the time we're finished, she's bleeding and crying and I rush upstairs and yank down my pants and masturbate for the first time in years.

Outside, a coyote howls and a jet roars overhead.

NOSTALGIA

I'm at the kitchen table finishing off the last of the garbage loaf when somebody knocks on the door. I think about ignoring it but, again, the paranoia.

It's the blond guy again, Big Cigarette. He has food or puke or possibly blood encrusted on his chin. I think about offering him a cigarette but decide not to.

I open the door and tell him I don't have any cigarettes.

He shakes his head and says, his voice weird, "Need a stamp."

"What happened to you?"

He holds up a bloody bag I hadn't noticed and says, "Pulled all my teeth. Now I gotta ship em off but I ain't got no stamps."

"Let me check." I back away from the doorframe and he steps into the house. I decide not to stop him. I do nearly everything online and can't remember the last time I mailed anything. It was before Ann died, for sure. Actually, that isn't true. The last time I mailed something was when I mailed one of Kasey's teeth to Rumble. So apparently the only thing you need stamps for now is to mail teeth.

"Smells like garbage loaf in here," he says and I hope he isn't moving toward the kitchen. I'm confident screams cannot be heard from outside the house, but they are still detectable from within. Kasey's screaming a lot right now. Probably because of the fried slab of garbage loaf I tied to the bottom of her foot although, in all honesty, it shouldn't even really be that hot anymore. This reminds me I need to complete this transaction quickly so I can get back to the garbage loaf. It's only edible if you fry it up and eat it while it's still warm, preferably in sandwich form.

I rummage through the old desk where Ann used to sit and pay bills and am surprisingly overcome with a rush of nostalgia. I locate a book of stamps and walk back out to the living room where the guy sits on the couch nodding off, his bag of extracted teeth sitting on his lap.

"Here you go, man" I say. "I need to get back to my dinner."

He snaps awake and stands up. "Would you mind if I hung around? Took a nap?"

"Sorry. I gotta head out in a bit."

His head perks up a little and he says, "You hear that?"

"No. What?"

"Sounds like somebody screaming."

I smile and say, "That's just the girl I have in a cage in the basement. That's the main reason you can't stay."

"Whatever. That fat lady with all the dogs said this house screamed a lot."

"That's Kim Barrel. She's crazy."

I hold the screen door open and he finally leaves.

He reaches the edge of the yard, roughly where he puked before, and says, "It okay if I take a nap here?"

"I don't care," I say, shutting the door and getting back to the garbage loaf.

After finishing the garbage loaf, I feel like I have to go somewhere because I told the guy I had to. It's still daylight out, early evening, so I decide to make a surprise visit to Lisa. After that, I need to see if that store has any more garbage loaf. I'm kind of addicted to the stuff and it's very affordable. The guy's still asleep in the yard and I imagine someone will think he's ODed and call the cops on him. I contemplate making a sign that says, "Not ODed. Just napping," before deciding I don't really care that much and, I don't know, it's entirely possible he has ODed and needs serious medical attention.

THE RUDY RUMBLE BUSINESS

When I get to Lisa's, her car isn't in the driveway. I go to the door anyway, thinking maybe she's parked in the garage or left Austin with Harold. I'm really just here to see Austin. I should have called first.

I ring the doorbell and Harold answers the door, wearing a fishing hat and multi-pocketed vest, looking boring.

"Lisa and Austin aren't here right now," he says.

"Yeah. I should have called first."

"You look all beat up."

"It's no big deal," I say. "I got jumped outside Walmart."

"Jeez. Black guys?"

"No . . . it wasn't black guys. At least, I don't think it was. I didn't see them. What . . . does that even matter?"

"You're right," he says. "I guess it doesn't. It's just that most crimes are committed by blacks."

"You know that's not true, right?"

"You have your reality. I have mine. That's what people are saying these days, isn't it?"

Are they? I don't know. I've only ever thought about my reality.

"Did they catch the guys?" He quickly shakes his head. "Of course they haven't. If they had, you'd know for sure they were black. Can we at least agree they were probably men? Women don't do things like that."

"I'm sure they do sometimes but I would agree with you on that. A man or men probably did it."

"You shaved. Cut your hair. I almost didn't recognize you."

"It's so hot out. I thought I could save some money on air conditioning." If there was one thing Harold could understand, it was economizing.

"Good idea. You're getting too old to look like that anyway."

This kind of hurts. I never understand why people think it's okay to insult the former version of a person. They're still insulting that person. But what am I going to do? Punch him in his boring round face?

Instead I just smile and say, "I'll never be as old as you."

"That's true," he says. "Another thing we can agree on." He pauses and checks his watch. "Well, I was heading out to do some fishing. You're welcome to wait around here or you can come with me. I can get another rod out of the garage."

My first instinct is to say no but I'm agreeing to go with him before I can think of a good reason not to and then we're in his truck and driving out to Gethsemane where one of his cousins owns a farm with a lake on it and we're mostly silent the entire time and then we're both in a small boat in the middle of the lake, a pond really, and the evening sun is beating down on us and it's quiet except for the sound of insects and birds and the distant laughter of his cousin's grandkids playing in the yard surrounding the house and I feel almost unnervingly peaceful then stupid, boring, fat Harold ruins everything by saying, "You need to stop it with the Rudy Rumble business."

I nearly drop my pole in the water. "What . . . uh, what are you talking about?"

There's no change in his expression or body language and I wonder if Harold even has a pulse. He never takes his gaze off the line penetrating the water.

"I just hope you haven't done anything that can't be undone."

I'm still trying to wrap my head around Rudy Rumble's name coming from Harold's mouth. I have to remind myself that Rumble is not just a monstrous drug dealer, part-time pimp, drunk, sexual deviant, and maker of weird music, out there stalking the night in his black rape van. He's also the Parking Lot King. An upstanding member of the community. One with, presumably, a fair amount of influence.

"I still don't know what you're talking about," I say. I just want to see him react in some way, even if it's only to grow outraged.

"I didn't let on. Just so you know. I handle Leonard Thigpen's taxes. He just happened to casually ask if I knew you one day when he called with a question. Then it just kind of all fell into place. Lisa's been telling me some things too. I told her about the Leonard business. She's really the one that put it together. If you keep it up, it's not gonna end too good. Besides . . . Ally's gone, you know? We all miss her but nothing's going to bring her back. Now, I don't know what you've been doing or if you're planning something but . . . I don't know, the world doesn't need any more of that stuff. Find some other way to get through this. Think of the world you want Austin to grow up in."

I think, *A world without Rudy Rumble*, and say, "What did you say when he asked if you knew me?"

"Not much. Just told him you were my brother-in-law. I think he already knew that."

"You didn't tell him Austin was staying with you, did you?"

Then he shoots me a glare and I realize, with my question, I've just confirmed his and Lisa's suspicions. The look he shoots me says, "Do you think I'm an idiot?" but he already knows the answer to that and says instead, "He never asked. It never came up."

I clear my throat as if to say something and then say nothing.

"I don't want to keep talking about this," he says. "Just . . . I hope you're not in over your head. It would kill Lisa to lose you too."

I sit in the tiny boat, occasionally glancing at Harold's serene face, and realize I completely misinterpreted what he was talking about. He and Lisa don't think I'm stalking Rumble for vengeance. They would never suspect that I have his daughter locked in a cage in my basement. They think I'm using drugs. That's what that whole conversation was about.

I think about kicking Harold out of the boat and rowing to the shore of the pond and running back home and think about how ridiculous that would look and that I'm probably too tired to do anything like that anyway. Instead, I sit in the boat with him for a couple more hours. He's tranquil. I'm seething. Neither one of us catches anything.

We stop at a McDonald's on the way back to his house and eat inside and it feels like I'm back in the break room of the factory.

Lisa and Austin are back and Austin doesn't recognize me and it takes him a while to warm up to me and by the time I leave I'm convinced he didn't know who I was the entire time and, to his little baby brain, that bearded and long-haired guy who took care of him from time to time is gone and it makes me wonder why we bother doing anything.

On the way back home I stop by the store and buy cigarettes and garbage loaf. I pass Kim Barrel standing in her front yard with three of her dogs on leashes. I'm pretty sure one of them is dead.

.

FILLING EMPTINESS WITH EVIL

Kasey sits in the cage. She can barely lift her head or open her eyes. She was fairly thin to begin with but she looked healthy and possibly even a little athletic. That has all been stripped away. Her ribs and sternum are plainly visible behind her small breasts that now hang like half-filled water balloons. Her knees bulge against the tight skin of her legs. The stinking hunk of garbage loaf is still tied to her foot. The good thing about all the opiates is that she's stopped shitting in the cage. She's covered in scrapes and cuts and bruises and it hurts me to look at her because all I see is Ally. I think about what Harold said about nothing bringing Ally back. There's truth to that, sure. I know I don't have to be doing this. I know this is wrong. But I also know Ally's death tore a giant hole somewhere deep inside of me and whatever desire I had to do good escaped my body through that hole and the terror and misery I'm building in my basement is somehow filling that hole. Maybe it's better to be filled with evil than to be empty.

"It's almost over," I say and I'm not really sure if I'm talking to Kasey or myself.

She almost falls over and slowly crawls to the side of the cage nearest me.

"Where is it?" she says.

"Where's what?"

"The pills. Where are they?"

"I don't really have much left."

"You're not going to do this to me, are you?"

"You'll get them all before it's over."

"I'll do whatever you want. I'll suck your cock. Let you fuck me. I won't even try to get away."

I think of those words coming out of Ally's mouth and my self-righteous resolve is immediately restored.

She's clutching the bars of the cage, her knuckles scraped and bleeding. "Please listen to me," she says. "I know what you're trying to do but . . . my dad is not you. I know you lost your daughter and maybe you were a good person before that and you want him to go through what you went through but he won't. He just won't. He's not even capable of it. He probably *wants* me gone. You're doing what he wants. Just let me out."

She's blubbering now and I have to get out of the basement before what she's saying starts to make any sense. Besides, I tell myself, it isn't true. She's in desperate junkie mode right now. She'll say anything to get what she wants.

ALL THE GOOD IN THE WORLD CAN DISAPPEAR IN A SECOND

I head to the store for cigarettes. The day is clear and warm with an edge of crispness hinting at fall.

Kim Barrel's out in her front yard and I think I probably should have just driven or at least cross the street and hope she doesn't notice me. But it's too late.

"Hey, Hamm's Man," she calls and cackles. "Got any more Hamm's for me? Mama needs her some Hamm's!"

She's acting really wild. Like a homeless person who owns a house. I don't even know how she, of all people, can recognize me so easily. I decide not to talk to her.

"Look at him," she says to no one or her dogs. "Big Hamm's Man's too fucked up to talk." Then she just starts shouting "Hamm's Man! Hamm's Man! Hamm's Man!" like a football coach yelling at his players.

From behind me there's the roar of a car and, from the window, "Hey, lady! I'm gonna fuck your dogs!"

I keep walking. My blood is already up and I just want to get away from this so I can at least have a few minutes of silence away from the horror show in my basement.

The car slams on its brakes and backs up. It's a Mustang covered completely in some sort of reptile skin decal.

I've now moved beyond Kim Barrel's house but have to stop and turn to watch.

A guy emerges from the driver's side of the car. I'm pretty sure it's the clerk from the hotel but . . . I don't know. A lot of people look kind of the same to me.

"Lady," he says. "Those dogs are dead."

"You stay the fuck away from me now. You hear?" Kim Barrel looks terrified.

The man draws closer to her. He moves slowly, lazily, and I'm now convinced he's the guy from the Dayton Palace. He seems vaguely menacing but not angry in an overt kind of way.

"That dog is dead." He points to one of the dogs Kim Barrel has been dragging around the front yard. "That dog is dead." He points at a second one. I think it's the cocker spaniel. "That one, I will fuck."

The living dog is furiously barking at him and Kim Barrel is kicking out one trunk-size leg and I don't even think I care what happens so I turn and keep walking toward the store and that Ken guy is on his porch and I nod at him and he nods back and a couple minutes later the Mustang roars down the street, a dog's head hanging out of the passenger-side window, tongue wagging and happy.

Thankfully, by the time I buy my cigarettes and come back around, Kim Barrel has gone inside. The man in the car must have convinced her the dogs were dead because they are still out in the yard and I imagine coyotes will remove them once the sun goes down.

A couple doors from my house, my phone vibrates.

On the rare occasion this happens it's usually a robo-call but I pull it out to make sure it isn't Lisa.

It's Lisa.

She sounds panicked.

"Did you take Austin!" she shouts.

At first, the question doesn't even register. When it finally does, it sends my heart racing, the pressure roaring in my ears.

"What?" All the moisture has left my mouth and my voice is a dry croak.

"I can't find Austin!"

I've continued walking through all of this and am now right up on my house.

I instinctively glance at the mailbox and if I'd ever thought there was as much as a microscopic grain of good in the world, I knew I no longer would from this moment forward.

    "I think I found him," I say.

    Blood drips from the mailbox.

NUMB

It's like I don't have time to grieve, not even for a second.

I'm probably just being overly paranoid, but I have to do something with Kasey before the cops get here.

First, I reluctantly dose her—I'd wanted to begin the cold turkey withdrawal phase of the program—and she acts like someone who has just discovered the most beautiful mysteries in the universe and she'd probably do anything I asked her to but I'm still too paranoid so I duct tape her mouth and all around her arms and legs and stuff her in a sleeping bag and dump her in the attic behind a wall of boxes.

I should dismantle the cage but that would take too long and it isn't illegal to have a cage in your basement. Just creepy and suspicious as fuck. I don't use the hose to clean up the area because I don't want it to look like I've hastily concealed a crime scene, which is exactly what I'm doing. I use some damp towels to give the floor a wipe-down and make sure there's nothing too damning lying around. If they ask about the cage I'll just look embarrassed and tell them I sometimes use it for sex stuff and figure they probably will not ask me any further questions.

A single cops shows up and I think that, in and of itself, is a bit odd. Lisa was the one who called and I have no doubt she adequately conveyed the severity of the situation. The cop is one of the guys at Handstands the night the Beach Boy died. He was one of the ones wearing wraparound shades and a lot of camouflage. One of the hunters.

He wears black latex gloves and, even though it's still daylight outside, he pulls out his flashlight and shines it in the mailbox.

I feel sick and my head is reeling and I think this has to be the end. Rumble's gang has figured out that Kasey is here and they've done this heinous thing to Austin to give the cops an excuse to search the premises and find her and all of a sudden I'm the bad guy. I'm the one going to jail for kidnaping and probably rape.

"You say you just came back and found it here?"

"Yeah." And I don't care how professional this guy is, or how much of a monster he is, the fact he is not showing a single shred of empathy or emotion, the fact he doesn't seem disturbed or put off by a mutilated baby in a mailbox, seems completely unreal to me.

"And where did you go?"

"The Superette to buy some cigarettes."

"How long were you gone?"

"Maybe forty-five minutes, tops."

"Did you check the mailbox before you left?"

"I don't remember. If I did, it wasn't like this. I probably did."

"So this happened while you were away?"

"Yeah."

He clicks the flashlight off and transfers it to his belt. He walks to his cruiser, opens the trunk, and pulls out a square of clear plastic. He returns to the mailbox and flaps the square of plastic open until it's nearly large enough to cover my stoop. He then reaches his hands into the mailbox and extracts Austin's mutilated corpse before placing it on the tarp.

"And you believe this is your missing grandson?"

I can't even look at it. I feel like I need to sit down. I can't sit on the stoop because I don't want to be that close to it. I dazedly drift over to a tree in the front yard and sit down heavily, leaning against it.

"Yes," I say.

It's not hitting the cop the same way. I'm watching him as he crouches to paw the corpse.

"What we have here are not human remains."

It takes me a second to process this. I really didn't think there was any questioning it. Austin goes missing. There's a mutilated carcass in my mailbox that, to me, looks exactly like a baby or at least something that had been a baby before its skin and some of its limbs were removed. This has to be Austin, right?

"What?" I say.

"You can come take a look if you want. It's a skinned cat. Or maybe a dog. I dunno. This isn't your grandson, though, I'm happy to say. It's not a human. Never was."

I struggle to stand up. I'm thinking of other scenarios now. Maybe it is some kind of animal. Maybe Rumble has abducted Austin to sell him to some white slavery mill or something. I look at the corpse again. It's definitely a baby. It has to be Austin. And then I think this is just another sick prank. Like the cop is telling me this so I'll have to look at it, take in more of the detail than I did before.

"You're wrong," I say.

He places a large hand on my shoulder. A hand that was only moments before digging through the corpse of my grandson.

"I know coming home to something like this is a little . . . shocking. But we can't lose our heads over it."

"Get a coroner out here. Or a . . . forensics person or something."

He removes his hand.

"That would be a waste of money and resources. I've seen plenty of dead animals. Dead babies too. This is not your grandson. I think you're just a little out of sorts."

"So . . ." I'm fighting back tears. This all seems too unbelievably cruel. "That's it?"

"There really isn't any more I can do. If you want to file a report it might help if we happen to catch the person who did this. But we'd be looking at charging him with animal cruelty, maybe vandalism and menacing. Not murder, though. We already have people trying to locate your grandson. We'll find him."

"That really is it then?"

"I'm afraid so."

"You just come and do the least amount of work possible and see things how you want to see them and make a report and that's reality, right? That's what happened."

"Usually how it works, yeah. You're more than welcome to submit your own report. Like I said. We'll keep it on file. We have plenty of reports that make virtually no sense."

What good would it do? What would I even be fighting against?

What would the outcome be? Austin's already dead. I know this. The bloody pile of meat and bones currently adorning my stoop is the evidence. If this cop isn't even willing to accept that blatantly obvious fact, how can things move forward from there? Arguing with him about whether or not that is my grandson or a fucking skinned cat seems so absurd and hopeless that I just want him to go away. He's the crazy one. It's just that his craziness is sanctioned by a greater institution and that makes it socially acceptable.

He pulls out a stick of gum and unwraps it with his gore-covered gloves before folding it into his mouth.

"I can go get the paperwork out of the cruiser if you want to write up that report."

The anger, the grief, everything feels like it has fallen away, replaced by numbness.

"Do you feel good about what you do?" I say.

"I've always wanted to protect and serve my community. Ever since I was a kid."

I think about asking him what his definition of community is because I guess he's serving his immediate community of friends very well, so he isn't lying.

"You're all fucking monsters," I say. "Does it make you feel good to be surrounded by broken people? Job security, I guess."

"*Okay,*" he breathes out. "I think I'm done here."

He begins walking toward his cruiser.

"Aren't you going to take the remains?"

"I can get you the number of an animal control service. They'll get rid of it for you, if you don't want to deal with it."

I can't say anything to that.

SENSE OF HEAVEN

I'm walking down my street toward Kim Barrel's, Austin's remains in a black, heavy duty trash bag. While wrapping him in the tarp, surrounded by the fading sunlight and gathering coolness, happy kids laughing in yards, angry adults yelling and slamming doors, the sounds of distant cars on the highway, cooking smells coming from people's grills and exhaust fans, it's like I entered a different world. I should say I felt like I'd reached the lowest level of a world I'd entered soon after Ann died. Even after seeing the girl run over in front of my house and deciding to do what I set out to do, it still felt like my descent into that world was governed by some shred of rationality. A sense of justice. A desire to restore balance even if, ultimately, that balance was only within me. Until now, I'd also felt the need for some sort of self-preservation so I'd have the ability to follow through with my plan. So that I could remain in Austin's life.

I no longer have that.

This thing has to end.

I don't care if it's quiet or loud and violent. I don't care if I'm the only one who knows or the whole world ends up knowing. I don't care if I fail or die trying. I can't sit around anymore.

I smell smoke before coming up on Kim Barrel's house and noticing it's the one burning, completely engulfed.

Ken stands on the sidewalk in front of her house, watching it with a bemused expression on his face before taking a long, slow drag from an unfiltered cigarette.

He glances at me, nods toward Kim Barrel's house, and says, "Burnin."

I don't even think about reaching for the phone in my pocket and calling 911.

"Don't think we've met," he says. "I'm Drifter Ken." He holds out a filthy hand and I take it.

"I'm—" I start to say but there's a shift in the breeze, blowing smoke in my face and then I'm coughing and coughing.

"It's okay," Drifter Ken says. "I'd probably forget it anyway."

I manage to catch my breath and straighten up and he's the first to spit out a stifled laugh and it shatters the last grain of sanity I have in me. As Kim Barrel's house burns, we stand out on the sidewalk and neither one of us can stop laughing and I realize Drifter Ken has the same sickness I do. He's probably been living with it a lot longer than me.

"She was over at my house just a while ago," Drifter Ken says. "Real upset about somethin. Said she was gonna go home and hang herself and I said there wudn't nothin gonna hold her. Guess she took my advice and opted for immolation."

And this sets us off on another round of laughter.

"That bitch'd do anything for a case of Hamm's. Sucked a pretty mean dick too," he says, taking a final drag from his cigarette and flicking it toward the house.

He asks what I have in the bag and I tell him and he says, "That ain't right." Then he tells me he recognizes that wild look in my eye and that I'm about to start a journey and that I need to have one more night to myself before I commit my soul to vengeance and anger and I agree with him and I go back home and put the trash bag of Austin's remains on the kitchen table and pocket the bottle of oxies I was saving for Kasey and get into the car and drive to a hardware store where I buy a garden claw and then I go through McDonald's because I think if I eat something maybe I'll stop shaking and there's a Cadillac in front of me at the drive-thru and the driver is offering the worker fifty bucks if she'll show him her tits and she tells him this isn't a strip club and besides she'd get fired if she ever did something like that because everything is being recorded all the time and I get my food and eat in the parking lot and pop one of the oxies when I'm finished and I throw all the trash out the window and it feels like I'm sliding into a cool sleeping bag and I mess with the dial on the satellite radio until I hit something that feels lavender soft and fuzzy and wordless and I'm driving around all night, listening to music and popping pills until it feels like my insides are scrubbed out, until it feels like my viscera has been removed, and I'm just a brain living in that world that has nothing but muted pastel colors and no sharp edges and I've never really had much of a sense of heaven but this feels really close and then I'm seeing the fading neon of downtown in the rearview mirror and I'm lifted from unconsciousness by the violent sun rising from behind my garage and I'm in my car and all the windows are up and I'm sweating and it stinks because I've puked all over myself and I think, *This is the real world*, and I should go inside and go to bed but I'm not going to. I don't want to sleep until this is over.

THE CHILDREN OF MONSTERS

I restore Kasey to the cage in the basement. I now smell so bad myself I don't even notice how bad she smells.

She seems fundamentally changed in some way.

There's no begging or pleading or anything. It's how a person looks when they know they've lost the fight.

"I need you to eat something," I say.

"Not . . . not hungry," she says.

"It's not an option."

I shove the trash bag through two bars of the cage, grab hold of the bottom, and shake its contents out, Austin's corpse hitting the cement floor with a heavy splat.

Kasey recoils slightly.

"What . . . what is it?"

"It's my grandson, Austin. Someone left him in the mailbox."

"It wasn't my dad. It was probably Lenny. I'm telling you, my dad doesn't care enough to do that."

"All of this is unimportant. You're going to eat it because I want you to."

"Are you going to . . . to give me something if I do?"

This is what I was talking about before. The fundamental change. Maybe it's how a person acts when all sense of pride has left her.

"That . . . can't be part of it," I say.

"Why not?" she practically whines.

"When trauma changes a person, do you think life is worth enough to keep on living? Or should we just pack it up?"

"I don't know what you mean."

"Like . . . do you think if I let you go, you could ever be the same?"

"No. But maybe I didn't like who I was."

"Okay. Fair. Do you think you could ever experience joy or happiness, having been through what you have?"

"Yeah. In what ever way possible."

"Really?"

"You're forgetting who raised me. I would have killed myself when the idea first occurred to me if I thought something like trauma would prevent me from enjoying life."

This gives me pause. I've been thinking of Kasey as average and she's anything but. The children of monsters are covered with calluses and scar tissue but, beneath that, there is a conscious being capable of constructing her own life.

"Supposing I let you live . . . do you want to live the rest of your life knowing you voluntarily ate a baby's corpse for drugs or would you have rather done it because you were *forced* to do it?"

She fixes her gaze on me and, for a second, I think she's just been fucking with me. There's so much clarity in her expression it almost feels like I'm playing *her* game.

"Nobody wants to be forced to do anything. I will always choose free will."

Suddenly I'm furious and I'm reaching for the whip and the shepherd's hook and holding her head down over the corpse, the hook behind her neck, and she's so raw from the lack of pills that her pain is magnified and she's sobbing as she takes bites of the flesh and I tell her I'm going to go take a shower and do some things and when I get back I want to see nothing but a pile of clean bones and tell her that maybe, *maybe*, if she can manage to do that I might have a couple pills left to give her and tell myself that if I come back to realize she hasn't bothered taking another bite then I'll let her go.

SOFT TUNES UNDER THE FULL MOON

It's late in the summer and the sun is savage and intense.

There's a glossy flyer taped to my door, its edges curled from the brutal heat.

It's black and purple and in soft focus.

It's an ad for an event called "Soft Tunes Under the Full Moon."

Featuring:

The soft synth tunes of a solo Rudy Rumble.

A monthly drawing.

Lenny's Famous Fun Room.

Free Balloons!

Where: The parking lot of the old K-mart at the corner of Woodman and Burkhardt.

It starts at ten o'clock tonight.

On the back of the flyer someone has written, "Thot u mite B intrestd," and they've signed it as, what looks to me like, "Bremj." Bremj must be my new toothless, smoking friend.

I go out to the garage and make a new weapon.

HUMANITY

Hours later, I go down to the basement to find that Kasey has eaten all of Austin.

She looks at me, her mouth crusted with blood, and says, "You said you might have something?"

"I lied," I say and bask in the screams from Kasey, laugh as she jams fingers down her throat, trying to bring up everything she can. While vomiting, a large amount of discharge drops from her ass and vagina and I realize she has stuffed a large part of the corpse inside of her because that was easier than actually eating it. My faith in humanity is not restored.

THE SECRET LIFE OF PARKING LOTS

The parking lot of the abandoned K-mart is filled with cars. A number of people are approaching the lot on foot. It looks like most of them are on their way to a festival or something—couples, groups of young people, some older people, children, some people pushing strollers. It's kind of a trashy area and most people look like they come from around here, their sense of fashion ranging from the late eighties to the early aughts. I'll fit in easily.

I park my car in the first spot I can find and get out. I have a new weapon slid down the left leg of my pants and initially try to hide my limp until I notice nearly everybody around me has a limp of their own.

There's a high makeshift wall erected at the halfway point in the parking lot. It looks like the panels are just twelve-foot tall sections of drywall that have been painted in awful pastel colors and, after stepping through the opening, it feels like I'm at some sort of beach club. There's a small stage in front of the vacant storefront, a tropical-themed mural erected at the back of it.

A family is coming up behind me—man, woman, and small boy. The boy seems upset, the dad looks zonked, and the woman says, "Calm it, Cody. Just let Mommy and Daddy relax for a little bit."

Without realizing it, I'm standing in a line. Rather, a loose line has formed. Most people look angry or dazed. The signage isn't very good. Other than the stage, there's no real indication of why anyone is here.

There are a few young women who have the air of nurses about them wandering amongst the sloppy herd of people and saying something to them. Once the women move on, the people either move up closer to the stage or just kind of further assimilate into the line.

A sign goes up toward the front of the line:

GET YOUR FREE BALLOONS HERE

I don't really see any balloons though and imagine someone furiously working the helium tank at some hidden location. Maybe they want to bring them out all at once so it's more dramatic.

Another nurse woman stands at the front of the line, under the sign, a large trash bag on the pavement beside her. Behind her stands a large man with guns on either hip. The man at the head of the line hands her his driver's license, she takes a photo of it with her phone, and hands him a tied off, uninflated balloon. The man shouts, "Thank you, Rudy!" before disappearing behind a white curtain. I let myself drift out of the line, feeling extremely naive.

It feels like I've discovered some secret life of parking lots.

There are easily a thousand people now either in the line or just milling around like they're waiting for something. I guess that's pretty much the life of an addict though. Waiting.

This all feels so temporary, like it would take less than an hour to disperse the crowd and tear down all the structures.

In front of the stage is a small booth that reminds me of a child's lemonade stand. The sign above it says, "ENTER OUR MONTHLY DRAWING," and there's a smaller line forming in front of it.

I drift to the end of the line, behind an extremely thin woman with dirty blond hair and a scab on the back of her neck. She's wearing pajama bottoms that look like they were purchased from the children's department.

"Excuse me," I say.

She turns slowly. She has another scab on her face and absolutely no life in her eyes.

"What's the drawing for?"

Her dead look becomes as dubious as it can and she says, "You serious?"

"Sorry," I say. "First time here."

She slowly looks me up and down and says, "I can tell."

"So help me out."

She kind of rolls her eyes and says, "First off, you get a free balloon just for entering your name. If you win . . . ." Her expression turns almost rapturous. "You get a *lifetime supply*." She draws those last two words out like it's all she wants out of life and, I don't know, it probably is. "So *that's* why I'm here."

"Yeah . . . uh, me too."

Then our conversation is pretty much over and I continue moving forward with the line, thinking I'll probably bail before I get to the front, especially if it involves showing a driver's license.

The woman in front of me gets twitchier and twitchier, pulling out her phone and drumming out texts with her gnarled fingernails. She hasn't turned the sound off on her phone and that annoying clicking effect works in concert with her fingers.

About twenty people from the front of the line, the woman in front of me turns and says, "You here alone?"

"Yep," I say. "Just me."

"What are you gonna do with your balloon? Is it for you or somebody else?"

"It's for me."

"You wanna give it to me? We can work out some kinda trade."

"Let me think about it."

"Don't think too long," she says. "There's about a hundred guys here who'd take me up on the offer."

A few more people enter the drawing and the woman in front of me keeps backing up into me, rubbing her bony ass against my crotch and throwing dead-eyed looks over her shoulder.

As we get closer, I see they *are* taking photos of driver's licenses but I'm not too concerned about it. This is all going to be over soon and there's part of me that wants Rudy Rumble to know I was here. I will have no choice but to act.

Now about five people from the front of the line, the woman turns around and doesn't say anything.

"Where we gonna do it?" I say.

"You got a car? If not, we can go around back."

"Will you come home with me?"

She looks lost for words. She glances at her phone.

"See," she says, "thing is, I got a husband."

"Yeah, you don't have to stay there all night."

She sort of shakes her hand holding the phone and puts it back in the pocket of her pajama pants.

"Okay," she says. "Here's the deal. You can enter whatever name you want to for the drawing. Also, you go through the main line and give me that balloon too. And there's one more chance for another free one. You give me those and enter my name in the drawing instead of yours or whoever's and I'll go home with you for a while. Not all night. I gotta get back home at some point."

"So you walk out of this thing with like six balloons." If I were actually a junkie, I'd feel like I was getting fleeced.

"Don't judge," she says.

"Girl's gotta do what a girl's gotta do."

"And you gotta let me fix before we do anything."

I smile as best I can and say, "You're probably going to need it."

I get to the front of the line, the hard-looking woman snaps a photo of my ID, and I slide the slip of paper I'm supposed to write my name and phone number on over to the woman who had been in front of me and hasn't left my side.

"So," I say to the woman running the booth, "if I *really* wanted to win the drawing, could I enter more times than once?"

"You can enter as many times as you want. Write down whosever name you want. Each additional entry's ten bucks."

"Do a lot of people do that?"

"Not really. Most folks don't have the money."

"Do you remember the last person who did?"

"Sure do," the woman laughs.

"Oh yeah?"

"She wasn't entered for herself. She was puttin in somebody else's name. Ally uh . . ."

"Yeah, yeah," I say. "Do you know who it was?"

"Damned if I remember her name. I'm pretty good with the names of the winners but I can't remember everyone who comes through here. Only thing I remember about her was she wore probly one of the worst wigs I ever seen." The woman laughs again. "I mean, it was really unflattering."

At this point, there's not even anger left inside me and I'm surprisingly unsurprised.

"Well, got a long line," the woman behind the counter says.

I slide the slip of paper to her, noticing the woman who I'll be spending my evening with is named Kitty Bender, and I think that sounds like some sort of carnival act.

"So what now?" I ask Kitty.

"Next up is Lenny's Fun Room."

She's already headed off in the direction of another makeshift structure, this one a large black box the size of a small garage. There's a black curtain for a door and there are bright flashes of light licking out from under the curtain.

I grab Kitty's arm and say, "Wait. Maybe we should do the main line first."

"But it's so long."

"We'll go out to my car and you can . . . do whatever you need."

She looks toward Lenny's Fun Room and wrinkles her face. "Yeah. It's probably better to wait anyway. That guy creeps me the fuck out."

We walk back to my car and Kitty sits in the passenger seat and she's very quick and after she sticks herself she asks why I'm not doing anything and I tell her I want to be able to get it up later and she completely understands this. She doesn't ask why my seat is slid all the way back to accompany my unbending left leg. Maybe she's just used to deformity and injury.

"I didn't do much," she says. "I don't want you to think I'm gonna be nodding off or anything."

"I'm not too worried about it."

We get out of the car to go stand at the back of the long line. It moves slowly and Kitty spends most of the duration leaning against me so she doesn't fall down. There's something about this gentle contact that feels like the calm before the storm so I don't really mind it.

It's now completely dark. The only lights in the parking lot are the bright neon lights coming from the stage. About halfway through the line, a man in a suit walks on to the stage, approaches the microphone, and says, "Ladies and gentlemen, welcome to Soft Tunes Under the Full Moon. I'm very pleased to announce . . . *Rudy Rumble!*"

And Rudy Rumble walks out wearing baggy khaki slacks and a white and peach-colored sweater, despite the heat.

He moves the mic behind the keyboard, setting it down to a howl of feedback.

When the feedback fades, he leans into the mic and says, "Are you guys ready to relax!" and there's a smattering of drugged-out applause that doesn't seem to diminish his enthusiasm at all.

He flips some buttons on the keyboard and starts poking some keys and suddenly the parking lot is awash in deafeningly loud elevator music.

Kitty grabs my hand and says, "I love his shit so much," and it almost feels romantic.

Once we get closer to the front of the line, Kitty's phone is again in her hand and she's typing in texts and making angry faces.

She stuffs the phone into her pajama pants, looks at me, and says, "I don't know why he doesn't just put him to bed. It's past his bedtime anyway."

"Sounds reasonable," I say.

"You got any kids?"

"Nope."

"Don't do it," she says like she's not even aware how old I am.

"I think I'm a little past that."

Rumble's songs are all about a minute to a minute and a half, but as each one ends, it feels like an eternity has passed. Occasionally, a slow wave would gain momentum amongst the crowd and then the song would end and the people would continue moving until they realized it was a completely different song and then fall back into their confused shambling.

We move closer to the front of the line and it feels like I have something like a tuning rod running through the center of my body, vibrating gently.

Kitty pulls her phone back out and looks at it again.

"He wants me to come home," she says.

"Who?"

"My husband."

"Do you want to go home?"

"No. It's my night out."

"Then don't. I'll take you home later."

"After you get what you want." There's something mean and derisive in the way she says this.

"You offered."

"You all just want one thing."

"I can hang on to my stuff. I'll take you home anyway."

She moves closer to me, now back to her idea of seductive. "Or you could give it to me anyway. Take a rain check."

"No." I point to the front of the line. "You're up."

She goes through the process and eagerly stands there waiting while I go through the process.

"To Lenny's Fun Room!" she says with more life than I've seen out of her all night.

"This one's a little different," she says. "You don't get it until after you go through."

"Is it like a funhouse or something?"

She wrinkles her face. "Not exactly. And you have to do it alone. I'll wait for you, okay?"

"Okay. You go first."

I'm immediately imagining the worst, Leonard sitting in a chair while people come through and suck his cock for heroin or maybe he just punches or beats each person coming through. Maybe he pisses on them or makes them eat shit. I think about all this as the armed man standing by the entrance lifts the ridiculous velvet rope to allow Kitty to pass through the black curtain. But then she's standing back at the rope less than a couple minutes later looking a little paler and somewhat shaken and then it's my turn and I realize the doorman is possibly the most stoned person here. That's good.

The music coming from Rumble is deafening, even in Lenny's Fun Room, and as soon as I step through the curtain I'm blinded by the clear white strobe light and walking through a narrow corridor that goes back about twenty feet before opening onto a stark white room, the strobe flashing, and it takes me a few seconds to process what I'm seeing. Leonard is in the room. He's wearing sunglasses, tight black men's bikini underwear, and nothing else. And he's dancing, not to the music, just dancing furiously and passionately and I think he's on way different drugs than everyone else here and then I take in what else is in the room and have to fight the urge to vomit.

A man sits strapped to a chair, something that looks like a beer bong protruding from his mouth, his stomach lumpy and distended. Beside the chair is a pile of teeth. Leonard is still dancing but now he's also pointing at the pile of teeth. I'm supposed to take one and drop it down the funnel. Kitty did this for a balloon of cheap heroin. Judging by the look of the victim's stomach, many other people have done it.

The tuning rod in my core is heating up, vibrating rapidly, and before I even think too much about it, my hand is on the garden weasel I've shoved down the left leg of my pants and I'm pulling it out and it's hard to focus on Leonard with the flashing strobe light and I hope he's having a hard time focusing on me too and he's stopped dancing and he's bending and reaching for something in his pile of clothes and I'm across the little room, jabbing out with the garden weasel, the stun gun affixed between the prongs, knowing it will work because I'd tested it out on Kasey, and the first jolt of the stun gun causes Leonard to stiffen up and drop to the ground and I hold it on him. Then I'm stabbing and twisting with the garden claw, trying to hit as many major organs as I can and then he's not moving and there's blood all over the floor but I don't think I have any on me and the whole thing was quick and silenced by the cacophonous synths of Rumble's music and I shove my weapon back into my pants and I'm standing at the entrance and collecting my balloon and putting my hand around Kitty's frail arm, really touching her for the first time, and saying "Come on, we need to get out of here," and she hesitates a little and I'm dragging her through the crowd and out to the car and she looks down at the cuff of my pants and says, "You're bleeding," and I don't say anything and by the time we reach my house I can tell she doesn't want to go through with this and she hesitates getting out of the car, saying "I've never done anything like this" like I'm just going to give her what she wants and drop her back off at her house with her bratty kid and shitty husband and I tell her I don't care, she can take it or leave it and go toward the house and she gets out of the car and follows me and I go down to the basement and she follows me, a look of horror creeping over her face when she sees Kasey crouched like a feral animal in the cage and I didn't think I was going to go through with this but I do and she lets me peel off her t-shirt and her pajama pants and her underwear and she takes me in her mouth and I press her face to the cage as I fuck her from behind, her body so frail and brittle it feels like I'm going to break her and Kasey stands up and is now face-to-face with Kitty and I focus on the heartbroken pity in Kasey's eyes while I explode into Kitty and pull out and tell her to get her clothes back on because I've got shit to do and tell her if she ends up getting pregnant she really needs to think about aborting that thing.

I WANT VENGEANCE

I'm back at the K-mart parking lot, parked a short distance away from the black van that is able to exist without license plates seemingly unmolested. Kasey's in the car with me. She smells atrocious and looks near death. She's unrestrained because, really, what's the point? The tuning rod running through me is ramped up again and it feels like it has thrown tendrils out to all my extremities and my insides are vibrating. I feel invincible. Feelings of invincibility inevitably lead to self-destruction but most people don't see it coming. I do. I see everything. I am the center of my universe. I have spent my entire life being an ostrich, keeping my head buried in the sand because to notice the things happening around me and to be bothered by those things meant I would have to do something about them and to exist at a very base level in a capitalist society means always stretching yourself thin, always overextending yourself. All I was able to do was make Ann more comfortable in her final days. If I hadn't retired early, I wouldn't have even been able to do that. I wish I had made enough money so we could have sought alternative remedies instead of attending appointment after appointment of what seemed to me like a highly ritualized and perfectly planned death sentence. The only thing I was able to do for Ally was watch Austin while she went out and got fucked up. I was hoping she would find a sense of purpose, one that made her embrace life and want to wake up in the morning. Neither one of us could have afforded the expensive rehab she needed, the kind that rewires the brain and has a chance of actually working. So I could only drive her to the Suboxone clinic, which is where she most likely found out about Rudy Rumble. There's always that question of time and money and most of us aren't cunning or vicious enough when we're younger to realize the only way we can achieve these things is to either have an excess of wealth or never get close to anyone. I would have given anything for what happened to Ann and Ally and Austin to have happened to me instead. But now I have no one and nothing to worry about so before I leave this world, I want to rid it of one less evil.

I'm out of the car and opening the passenger door and dragging Kasey out with one hand while the other clutches the stun claw. I jimmy one of the back doors of the van using a technique I found on YouTube and it feels entirely too easy and we're in the back of the van and, just as I was hoping, there are multiple things I can use to obscure Kasey with: a couple blankets, a blue tarp, a pile of clothes. In my brief observation, I'm somewhat astounded at how casual Rumble is about everything. Dangling from the rearview mirror is the chain and the shock collar. I just imagine rich white men reading about these atrocities online or in the paper and texting each other symbolic winks and back claps. After all, it's just thinning the herd, right?

Kasey is so thoroughly drugged she's barely conscious and when I tell her to lie down she lies down.

I crouch behind the passenger seat and cover myself with a foul smelling blanket. The windows are tinted so I'm not really that concerned with trying to conceal myself. I suppose the Leonard incident could make Rumble a little more vigilant but I'm not even really sure if the people entering Lenny's Fun Room after me would have cared enough to say anything. I probably should have freed the guy who was being fed teeth. It didn't really occur to me that people might go on feeding him teeth, even without Leonard's instruction. I feel like Rumble is more focused on what he wants to happen. This is the night he looks forward to every month. The full moon. Like a motherfucking werewolf or something.

I hear voices and then the passenger door opens and Rumble says, "Up you go. Congratulations, Miss Big Winner," and he sounds as casual as if whoever he's talking to just won a five-dollar scratch-off at the gas station.

The tuning rod through my center hums along even faster and

I'm imagining it beginning to glow.

The driver's side door clicks open and I spring across the seat.

Rumble takes a step back and his hand is in his pocket but I lurch forward with the stun claw, drilling him in the forehead with surprising accuracy. His spasm causes the small gun he was trying to extract from his pocket to go clattering to the asphalt. Now I'm out of the van, snatching up the gun and sliding it in my own pocket before anyone notices. I don't know what kind of gun it is. I don't know anything about guns. I know if you pull the trigger they go bang and sometimes hurt people. Maybe there's a safety.

Possibly it's the adrenaline surging through him, but Rumble is back on his feet quicker than I think he should be so I hit him with the stun claw again, this time on the chest where it opens his sweater and tears a gash in his skin. I kick-drag him closer to the van.

"Help!" he shouts. "Somebody help!"

I realize I've underestimated his ability to become a sniveling pussy in the blink of an eye.

Before I even know what I'm doing, I have the gun in my hand and I'm telling him to shut the fuck up and maybe he recognizes the look in my eye, maybe he sees I'm a gone man and I will most definitely shoot him before anyone has the chance to stop me because that tuning rod is glowing white hot and it would propel my body even if I didn't have a pulse.

And now he's just blubbering and I tell him to get in the van and he slowly climbs up into the driver's seat and I pull a set of handcuffs from my pocket and shackle him to the steering wheel.

Oddly, the woman still sits in the passenger seat and I can't really tell if she's in a state of shock or genuinely doesn't yet know what's going on.

I cross the front of the van to the passenger side and open her door and tell her to get lost, tell her she didn't win anything, I'm giving her a truly great prize, but she still doesn't move and I'm becoming a little concerned because Rumble is fumbling with his keys and trying to get them jammed into the ignition and the last thing I need is for him to drive away, so I physically drag the woman from the van.

She dazedly wanders away and absently extracts her phone from her pocket.

I hop into the passenger seat and say, "Find us a nice quiet stretch of road."

"What do you want?" he says.

"I want vengeance," I say. "Now drive."

"Where do you want me to go?"

"Do you remember where you went four months ago?"

"I don't know what you're talking about. I'm all over the place every day."

"For now, just drive."

There are more than a few people milling about and I'm starting to get nervous.

"Don't think about asking anyone for help."

And it's like that force inside of me somehow reaches out and commands him to move. I'd like to think I would have shot him if he yelled for help but I don't know that I could have. And even if I shot *at* him there was no guarantee I would have hit him. It's almost like he knows he deserves what's coming to him.

As he backs out onto the street, nearly hitting a small child who is seemingly unattended, I say, "Give me your phone."

"Huh?"

"Give me your phone."

And I can tell by the way his face folds in on itself I've done the right thing. I hold up the stun claw to show I'm serious while turning in my seat to see if there's anyone following us.

Nothing looks suspicious.

"You wouldn't hit me with that while I'm—" he starts but I jab him in the leg and the van veers up onto the sidewalk and into some bushes.

"Give it."

He groggily reaches down and pulls a phone out of his pocket and hands it to me. I don't even bother checking to see if there's a tracking app on it. I know there is. I throw it out the window. I make him turn out his other pockets and another phone is revealed. This one also goes out the window.

Now he starts screaming for help in earnest and I drill him with the stun claw, hard enough to keep him quiet for a few seconds, and I reach between his legs, grabbing the lever that slides the seat back and I'm moving over and sitting on his lap, driving the van, just trying to get us away from here, and everything I do is instinctive. I try not to think about any of it.

I turn around and hit Burkhardt and begin driving toward downtown.

I feel him stir behind and beneath me and he's reaching frantically to his right in an attempt to grab the stun claw I've left abandoned, propped up against the passenger seat. His movement is restricted because of my presence on top of him and I grab the stun claw before he can. Then he's wrapping his arm around my neck and I think I remember in my research the power of the stun gun can not go through him and to me but since I modified it and jacked it up, I really don't know, so I slide my hand down to the middle of the metal shaft and drive the handle portion into what I think are his ribs until he relaxes his hold on me and I know I can't trust him to drive so I continue toward downtown in this ridiculous fashion, hoping a cop doesn't spot us. If so, I'm sure they'll recognize Rumble's plates-less van and come to his aid.

I'm looking for an abandoned area but this street is lined with old shitty houses. People are everywhere. On their porches and walking up and down the sidewalk. The only good thing is that hardly any of these people will call the cops if they see something strange.

I make a turn onto Fifth Street and continue to head toward downtown, realizing this seems counter-intuitive if I'm trying to avoid people. But Dayton was once a manufacturing town and most of that manufacturing has gone elsewhere. There are still places where gentrification has not yet reached its tentacles. We need more people to move here before the high-priced lofts and craft breweries can pop up this far out. When the houses turn into crumbling, abandoned buildings, I take a hard right and bring the van to a stop between a vacant lot surrounded by a chain link fence and a brick building with crumbling smokestacks and no windows.

Two cop cars turn onto the street behind me, each of them coming from different directions, and I immediately begin wondering if I have time to shoot Rumble and turn the gun on myself before they can stop me and then, curiously, they each make sweeping U-turns and drive away. I wonder how many sensors Rumble's van has on it and I wonder if it matters.

I realize I'm just doing something somebody else would have eventually done anyway.

When you build what Rumble has built, there's no solid foundation. It's the only way the illegal part of his ghetto empire could continue to exist. Nothing written down. Nothing made formal. To protect himself, it would all have to be made to go away in the blink of an eye, as quick as one of those booths in New York's Chinatown selling bootleg shit.

So these cops . . . they were probably already on their phones and radios, trying to figure out who was going to take Rumble's place, which one of them was going to be the naive sucker who wanted the power and the title as much as anything else. Because the smart ones, the truly dangerous ones, the ones who only want to profit, they're the quiet ones. They are the ones who stay out of the limelight, content with their cut. And when the shit starts to go down, they're the ones turning everyone else in to save their own hides.

To those cops, Rumble is already dead.

Their energies would now be put into mobilizing the troops, not rescuing a corrupt and greedy asshole.

And I don't feel a shred of empathy for him. I feel like a cat with a moth trapped under his paw.

Something hard and possibly metal smacks into the back of my head, turning my vision a blinding white, and my first thought is to wonder how Rumble did that when I can see both of his hands and then it dawns on me that I'm not completely wrong.

A Rumble did do it.

Just not Rudy Rumble.

Kasey Rumble.

Which is probably why the blow didn't incapacitate me.

I think, *Damn, this isn't how Stockholm syndrome is supposed to work.*

Then I'm turning toward her and pouncing on her, wrestling the tire iron from her and bringing it down across her legs. She's so high she probably doesn't feel any pain and I know the blow she dealt me was a one-shot deal done out of some sort of obligatory necessity more than any type of valid attack. In her current state, she probably wouldn't be able to stand up for five minutes, let alone defend herself in a physical altercation.

"Kasey?" Rudy Rumble says, his eyes framed in the rearview mirror.

"I'm sure you've been really worried about her," I say.

"I've had guys out looking for her since she went missing. I've been very worried."

"Bullshit," I say. "I was watching you every night until your friend Leonard took his frustrations out on me in the parking lot the one night. The only time I saw you look upset was when the old guy died."

"It's not the first time she's gone missing. She always comes back."

"She's not coming back this time."

I open the sliding side door of the van and drag Kasey out. She's not standing so well. I do my best to straighten her up and look her in the eye. I want to see something there. Hate, passion, fear, anything. What I see is nothing. Blank resignation.

I leap back into the van and grab the chain and the shock collar.

I put the shock collar around her neck and pull her close to me and whisper something in her ear, hoping it would ignite something in those dead eyes. I might as well have remained silent.

One end of the chain is through a ring in the shock collar. There's a latch on the other end and I'm at a loss as to what to do with it. I imagine Rumble fastens it under the front of the van but if I do that he's totally just going to gun it and—

Fuck.

Why didn't I turn the van off and take the keys?

Luckily, it's old and slow and heavy and I'm standing right by the sliding door so, at the first sign of movement, I hurl myself up into the van knowing Kasey isn't going far.

The van gains speed as I scramble to the front of it, grab the stun claw, and mercilessly lay into Rudy Rumble.

He loses all control while simultaneously mashing down on the accelerator and sending the van turning at what feels like a ninety-degree angle into the side of the brick building.

I'm thrown forward into the dash, my head smacking the windshield hard enough to crack it.

Rumble, not wearing a seatbelt, has been thrown into the steering wheel and bounces back into his seat. He clutches his chest with his free arm.

Thankfully, the van is still idling.

For a while, it felt like the tuning rod running through me was sputtering and bouncing all over the place but it's now once again humming along smoothly with that white hot intensity, burning away the panicked fog gathered in my brain.

"Where's the remote for the collar?" I say.

He nods toward the glove compartment.

I pull it out and hand it to him.

"Here's what I want you to do," I say. "I want you to drive over Kasey. I want to have the satisfaction of seeing you do that. If you'll do that for me—for *yourself*, because I know you need this to happen tonight, you need *your* fix—then I'll let you live. I'll disappear completely. Do you understand everything I've just said?"

He nods his head and what I see on his face tells me he's actually going to do this. The sick fuck is going to sacrifice his daughter to save himself and at that moment I feel so sorry for what I've done to Kasey. I feel sorry for her whole sad life and think maybe this is the best thing that can happen to her.

"Let's get to it," I say. "Before she can get away."

He backs the battered van out into the road. I imagine his cock is hard. He's not even trying to hide the excitement coursing through him. There's a wild, sparkling gleam in his eyes and I know he doesn't even see Kasey out there, bathed in moth-dappled fluorescent light, struggling to keep herself upright by leaning against the fence. His handcuffed left hand is clenched around the steering wheel while his right works the trigger of the remote.

A confused expression crosses his face and he angrily pokes the button harder and harder.

"It's not working because I never latched it," I say.

And, as if on cue, the collar falls from Kasey's thin neck and she turns to meet the glowing, injured glare of the van.

Rudy Rumble mashes the accelerator. There's a high-pitched whine and I'm not sure how fast the van can go. Kasey does her best to scramble away from it and I jam the stun claw into Rumble's neck and the van goes careening through the fence surrounding the vacant lot and this time, this time I remember to take the keys out of the ignition.

I know Kasey isn't going to bother us. I know she isn't going to get help. She's going to disappear into the night and that's where my thoughts about her will end. I can't think of anything more beautiful than that. A young woman swallowed by the humid, fragrant Ohio night to be reborn in the dawn as someone else.

I get out of the van and stand in the overgrown grass and weeds.

A rabbit hops along on the far perimeter. I take a deep breath. I'm going to miss Ohio in the summer.

I think about what I'm going to do. It's hard not to laugh. I haven't been this happy in years.

I pull open the driver's side door to find Rumble blubbering, trying to pull his hand through the cuff at any cost. The wrist is already swollen and bloody.

"Before we get started," I say, "I want you to tell me how you know my sister."

"I don't even know your fucking name," he hisses.

I tell him my name.

He tells me how he knows Lisa. It doesn't take long.

I spend the next two hours torturing him to death.

CURSED WITH HOPE

I stand on Lisa's front porch and alternately ring the doorbell and pound on the door. It's a couple hours before dawn.

The porch light flicks on and it seems way too bright but I don't even squint my eyes against it. I still feel invincible, like I can handle anything. The tuning rod running through me has melted. Still alive and vibrating, it has seeped into my blood and now it courses through my whole body and I feel like I'm glowing.

Harold cracks the door.

From behind him, I hear Lisa yell, "Who is it?" and Harold spits my name at her like a curse word.

Before Harold can say anything to me, I feel the need to compliment him on his porch. It's a beautiful porch.

"Did you . . ." I begin. "Did you stain your porch recently? It looks great. You built it, right? Look at the way the moisture just beads up on it. This thing's going to last forever. You're really good at doing things, Harold."

Lisa is there, pushing him out of the way. She's hastily put her wig on but it's sloppy and askew.

"Did you find him?" she says, frantic.

"Can I come in for a bit?"

"Have you heard anything? Why are you here? It's so late."

"I just . . . we need to talk about something."

She removes her burly physique from the doorway and I enter their house that smells like candles, boredom, and soul death.

I follow her into the kitchen where she immediately begins brew-

116

ing a pot of coffee.

Harold is behind me, sleepy and mostly unconcerned.

"I'd like to talk to Lisa alone, if you don't mind," I say.

Harold just stands there in the harsh light of the kitchen and blinks dumbly.

Lisa finishes scooping grounds into a filter, turns to Harold, and nods. It's as though she's powered him back on and he disappears from the room. I imagine him going into the spare bedroom, removing one of his guns from the gun cabinet, clipping in a round or sliding in a shell or whatever, sitting on the edge of the bed, and patiently waiting for a chance to use it. He probably thinks, to a certain extent, this is what his whole life has been building up to.

Lisa sits down heavily while the coffee brews.

I can't sit. I'm afraid if I sit down in this house, in this neighborhood, that I will not be able to get up again. I'm afraid it will wrap its narcotizing drywall and clean light and purified air around my abused body and whisper to me that here, I am safe, before plunging teeth into my jugular and greedily drinking all the blood from my veins.

I think there's a part of her that knows why I'm here. It's in the slump of her shoulders and the tilt of her head. Like she's waiting for me to hit her with a hammer.

"Why did you do it?" I say.

She doesn't answer right away, just stares into a middle distance while the coffeemaker slurps and gurgles and a train sounds its horn somewhere in the far distance. A tear escapes from her eye and rolls down a plump cheek, impossibly fast.

"I didn't do anything. Did you find Austin? We need to get our baby back."

I could tell her no one is going to find Austin. I could tell her what happened to him, try to traumatize her with that information, but I want her to have hope. Hope, unobtainable but forever yawning in front of her. I want that anxiety to eat away at her as she checks her phone every ten minutes for the rest of her life, while she sits down in front of the evening news with Harold. I want her to be plagued by the dark and sadistic imagination of the middle class.

"They'll find Austin eventually," I say. "The cop said they already have a few good leads."

I let her think about that but feel like there's a part of her that knows, because there's nothing at all hopeful in her expression. Maybe just . . . what? A realization she's made a deal with the devil and this is the fucking she hoped would never come?

"I'm going to go away," I say. "But first I need to know why you did it." I pause. "Or I at least need you to admit doing it."

She wipes away another tear and the coffeemaker finishes its brew cycle with a great sputter.

"I was desperate. Austin was in danger."

"Austin was fine."

"You don't know that. How could you know that?"

"We could have helped her."

"We tried. We tried everything we could." Now her face twists into something like anger and she looks me in the eye for the first time and I see the same bullying kid I grew up with, the same fat little girl who would steal my candy and sit on my chest until I couldn't breathe, the mask of the urbane, moral housewife falling away to reveal the confused and hateful creature underneath. "What? You think she was ever gonna change?" She tries to laugh ruefully but it seems too affected, like something she's seen someone do a million times on television shows but has never tried to pull off herself. "People don't change. You're an old man. You should know that by now. You need to get that through your thick skull."

She hasn't changed. I can see that.

"You're wrong," I say. "I've changed a lot. I've changed more than you could ever imagine."

"What did you do?" she says. Now something is rising within her and I can see the path this is going to take. She's going to turn this all around on me, try to make it my fault.

I have other things to do.

"I hope they find Austin," I say.

Now she's standing, sobbing and screaming "What did you do?" and I'm heading for the front door and Harold stands sadly in the doorway of the spare bedroom with a pistol in his hand, just as I'd thought, and as I close the door behind me I hear a loud gunshot and wonder if Harold has taken his own life or put my sister down like the sick, miserable animal she is.

I slide behind the wheel of my car and drive to the airport.

OCEANIC

This is the ending nobody wants.

I couldn't do it in my agitated state. It would have lacked meaning. If I had been possessed by some avenging spirit it would have felt like I was merely trying to kill it.

I had to let the agitation drain out of me.

I had to try and find happiness or something like it.

I flew to the Dominican Republic and checked in to a tacky all-inclusive resort in Punta Cana. It had three loud nightclubs that pounded music all night, every night, European tourists piling in and out. I never stepped foot in them.

I bought books from the hotel gift shop and listened to music on my phone and drank and smoked all day long while I sat on the beach and watched couples be happy around one another and families splash in the water and workers go about their business with smiles on their faces and I watched the clouds over the turquoise ocean and the sky darken and lighten and I tried not to think about anything because this was the end, the end nobody wants, and thinking about anything other than the right now was pointless but I couldn't stop myself from doing it, so I just tried to think about the good things that happened. There had been a lot of them and it lifted the heaviness that had flattened my heart.

Besides, thinking about the now was too seductive. It's always now. For someone like me, to have a future that would afford me the luxury of thinking about the now would have been an impossibility.

So . . .

I wake up and put on the thin cotton cargo pants I've bought specifically for this occasion, cinching the drawstring tight around my waist. I leave my phone and my book and wallet and everything else in the room. I have photos of Ann and Ally and Austin in my wallet but I can't look at them. Nor can I comfort myself with any Christian conceit that I will be joining them.

I go down to the beach where I pack my pockets with sand until it's a chore to walk. This fills me with a sense of purpose and no one asks what I'm doing, which is pretty grim against the riot of aggressive happiness around me.

I find a beach chair and sit down.

I sit there all day and most of the night.

Maybe I doze off periodically.

When I finally rise and walk toward the water, there's no one else around, almost like they're observing the solemnity of the situation and giving me some space.

I turn around to face the resort, the bright lights and the pounding music.

I want to drown myself in the ocean but I want to do it backward, turned toward the thriving cocoon of humanity rather than the indifferent waters of the endless ocean. I don't want to know where I'm going. I want to know where I came from.

I take my time, almost letting the tide rise around me, offering myself to the ocean, slowly easing back, the sand suctioning my feet. When the sky lightens and the neon from the hotel dies its quick death, I decide it's time. The water is filled with dead skin and dead minerals and dead fish and waste of all kinds. It feels like both the beginning and the end of all life on earth. I want to let the weight of it crush me and breathe it all into my lungs so I can finally feel at one with it. So I can finally rest.

Before the water takes me, I see a man standing on the beach.

I think he's waving at me.

I don't wave back.

Other Grindhouse Press Titles

Made in the USA
San Bernardino, CA
22 June 2019